The ONE for Me

ANNE SCHRAFF

SADDLEBACK
PUBLISHING

URBAN UNDERGROUND ®

SADDLEBACK
P U B L I S H I N G
www.sdlback.com

© 2013 by Saddleback Educational Publishing
All rights reserved. No part of this book may be reproduced in any form or by any means, electronic or mechanical, including photocopying, recording, scanning, or by any information storage and retrieval system, without the written permission of the publisher. SADDLEBACK EDUCATIONAL PUBLISHING and any associated logos are trademarks and/or registered trademarks of Saddleback Educational Publishing.

ISBN-13: 978-1-62250-042-0
ISBN-10: 1-62250-042-3
eBook: 978-1-61247-700-8

Printed in Guangzhou, China
NOR/0313/CA21300355

17 16 15 14 13   1 2 3 4 5

CHAPTER ONE

Jaris Spain, Kevin Walker, and Trevor Jenkins—three seniors from Tubman High School—were heading for their first class of the day. Suddenly, a gust of wind, called a "dust devil," blew up. The weather people had warned of Santa Ana winds, and dust devils could be expected. The boys held on more tightly to their binders lest a page blow away. But just ahead of them a girl was walking in a T-shirt and white denim shorts. The wind took the stack of papers she was carrying. As she dove to retrieve them, her shorts split in the rear, giving a clear view of her red panties.

Hearing the boys laughing behind her, the girl turned and screamed. "What are

1

you laughin' at, you freakin' fools?" She scrambled to recover more papers, and the split in the back widened, revealing still more of the red panties.

Jaris hadn't meant to laugh. In fact, laughing like that was out of character for him. It just happened, and he tried not to laugh. Kevin Walker, however, didn't try to stop. He laughed freely as the pretty girl tried futilely to pull her T-shirt down to cover the gaping tear in her shorts.

Trevor hurried to pick up some of the girl's papers, and Jaris and Kevin joined in. In a few minutes, they had recovered them all, but the girl didn't seem grateful. "You idiots just can't stop laughin', can you?" she screamed. As Kevin handed her the papers the boys had recovered, she demanded, "Do you laugh at automobile accidents too?"

"Hey, babe, cool it," Kevin urged. "Maybe next time you should buy a bigger size. Whatever size you're wearing ain't up to the job. Y'know what I mean?" He started laughing again.

"Oh, I could just rip that stupid smile off your face," the girl snarled. She was pretty, with an oval face and bright dark eyes that now crackled with hatred.

Trevor felt very sorry for the girl. He sympathized with how embarrassed she must be. Splitting your pants like that and revealing red lace panties was not a good thing, especially when teenaged boys were right behind you. Trevor was wearing a pullover sweater. On impulse, he yanked it off over his head. "Here," he said to the girl, holding it out to her. "Just tie the arms around your waist, and let the sweater hang down … the back … see? It'll cover … everything …"

The girl yanked the sweater from Trevor's hands as though he owed it to her. She tied the arms around her waist and stomped off, clutching her papers. She didn't even bother to thank Trevor.

"Now we can't see her red panties anymore," Kevin remarked. Another explosion of boyish laughter followed the girl like a taunt. "Darn you, Trev."

Then, as the angry girl disappeared around a corner, Kevin spoke. "Yet another member of the mean girls club. Maybe we should introduce her to Jasmine Benson. They'd make a great team."

"Who is she, I wonder?" Jaris asked. "I don't remember seeing her around."

Oliver Randall, another friend of the three seniors, came along just in time to hear Jaris's question. "Her name's Denique Giles," he offered. "She's just transferred from another school. I saw her filling out the papers in the office last week."

"Boy, Oliver," Kevin commented, "did you miss a show. It's probably the best thing that's gonna happen all day or maybe all week. A wind came up and blew her stuff away. Then when she dove to get it back, her shorts split. We all got to see her red panties."

Oliver laughed too. "You guys get all the breaks," he said.

"Never gonna see that sweater again, Trevor," Kevin warned. "You poor, good-hearted sap. It was a nice sweater too."

Alonee Lennox, Oliver's girlfriend, came along then. "You guys all laughing your heads off. What's funny?"

The four boys briefly looked at one another. Only Kevin was nervy enough to explain. "Well, Alonee, we saw this witchy girl just ahead of us. Her big behind was too much for her britches, and they split. We all got to see her red panties, and when we laughed in appreciation, she had a hissy fit."

"Oh brother!" Alonee groaned. "And here I thought you guys were too grown-up for stuff like that."

"It really was sort of funny," Kevin chuckled. "She's waltzing along, and the wind steals her papers. She makes a move to get 'em, and the shorts rip. Then the split widened, and we got to see even more." Kevin was still grinning.

"You too, Jaris?" Alonee asked, a smile on her lips. "Are you just a nasty little boy at heart too?"

Jaris shrugged. "What can I say?" He spread his hands out, palms up. "I just started laughing. It happened like spontaneously. Boy, was she mad, though. She looked like she coulda killed us all."

"Then this dummy Trevor pulls off his good sweater and gives it to that mean chick," Kevin went on. "And she ties the arms around her waist, and we couldn't see the show anymore. You know, Trev's sweater was kinda maroon, so it matched the red panties."

Jaris started laughing again. Alonee punched him, but not hard.

During lunch period that day, Denique went home to change her shorts. When she returned to the campus, she was wearing jeans. She looked around, searching for someone in particular. Denique was new on campus, but she knew Alonee Lennox from her English class. Alonee had helped get her up to speed in the reading assignments.

"Alonee! There you are!" Denique called out in relief.

"Hi," Alonee said.

"What a day I've had," Denique groaned. "This morning I stopped to pick up some papers that blew away in the wind, and my shorts split in the back. Just my luck a bunch of morons were behind me, and they started laughing like crazy. That's what comes of buying clothes in real cheapie stores, but what else can I do?" Denique's tone was bitter. "Anyway, there was this guy, he actually loaned me his pullover to cover my backside," Denique went on. "The others were absolute freaks, but he was civilized enough to try to help me. I don't know who he was. I didn't get his name. I wonder if you might know."

"Let's see," Alonee responded. Alonee recalled that Kevin had complained about Trevor ruining the red-panty show by loaning the girl his sweater. "That must have been Trevor Jenkins. He's a sweet guy. I ... ran into those boys you were talking about and they said Trevor loaned you his sweater."

Denique held the rolled-up maroon sweater. "Where's he now?"

"Trevor's in science, Denique, and I'm going there right now," Alonee answered. "I think you have it now too."

Denique looked at her schedule. She had science after lunch today. "Yeah, some guy named Buckingham," she noted. "I suppose he's as bad as all the other teachers in this crummy school."

"No, he's actually pretty good," Alonee objected. "You know, Denique, there are some good teachers here."

The two girls walked together toward science. "I was supposed to go to a private academy," Denique announced. "It's a really good school. But then my life fell apart totally. We lived in a nice house miles from this lousy neighborhood. Me and my sister had our own bedrooms, and we were both enrolled in the academy. There was no problem paying the tuition."

Denique grimaced. "Now we live in a dinky apartment, and Lindall and I have to share a room. And we're both stuck in this freakin' dump of a school."

Denique recited the sad tale with bitterness in every word. Alonee couldn't remember meeting anybody with so much anger in a long time.

"Well, I've *always* shared a room with my sisters," Alonee responded. "There are four kids in our family. Our parents got one bedroom, my brother has one, and we three girls share the big bedroom. It's not bad, though."

"Well, I hate it," Denique snarled. "Lindall, my sister, she's a freshman here, and she's into *all* my things. I never knew what a pest she was until I had to share a room with her. Nothing is off-limits to the little brat."

They neared the science classroom. Marko Lane and his girlfriend, Jasmine Benson, were outside talking. Marko eyed the pretty newcomer until Jasmine elbowed him. "Whatcha lookin' at, sucka?" Jasmine hissed.

Denique glared at Marko, who had been leering at her. She turned to Alonee and remarked, "There's another one! The boys at this school are *animals*. I was going to go to an all-girl academy, and it would've been so wonderful."

"Oh, I think I'd hate that," Alonee commented. "The boys make it fun here. I'd miss them in an all-girl school. Not that going to such a place was ever possible for us. My dad's a firefighter, and he makes good money. But we got six in the family, and money is tight."

"My father made good money too," Denique replied. "He's an engineer. But the dirtbag left us. Now Mom's struggling in a lousy little office job to keep us going." The girl's voice grew even more bitter. "Dad just skipped out. Doesn't even help us now."

"Oh, that's too bad," Alonee said sympathetically. She really did feel sorry for the girl. Alonee loved her father, Floyd

Lennox. She couldn't imagine him ever doing anything to hurt his family like that.

The girls entered the classroom, and Alonee pointed. "There's Trevor Jenkins. Is he the boy who—?"

"Yeah," Denique cut in. "That's him." She walked to the back of the room where Trevor was sitting. She didn't smile as she thrust the garment at him. "Thanks for loaning me this. Your friends are a bunch of creeps, but you're okay," Denique snapped.

Trevor took the sweater and mumbled, "I'm glad I could help."

Denique went back to where Alonee was sitting and took her place beside her. At the moment, Alonee Lennox was the only person at Tubman that Denique knew. She gravitated toward her like a port in a storm. "All the students here look creepy, like they're gangbangers or something," Denique whispered to Alonee before Mr. Buckingham came in.

"Oh no," Alonee protested, "most of them are good kids."

"Look!" Denique gasped. "There's one of those two who were laughing at me so hard they were choking!" She had spotted Jaris Spain. "Alonee, they were laughing just like maniacs when I had that accident. They were leering at me and ogling me. Oh, I hate them so much."

"Denique," Alonee whispered back, "I know that guy, and I know the guy he was with, Kevin Walker. They're both nice. Come on, you've laughed at something you shouldn't have laughed at. And then you regret it, right? Like maybe Grandpa spilled some soup on his tie or something. When my grandma's false teeth fell out one time, I laughed. I didn't want to hurt Grandma. I felt so bad because I love her."

Mr. Buckingham came walking in. He was a tall, majestic-looking black man whose ancestors were from the royal families of North Africa. He was dedicated to saving the environment. He was an excellent teacher and a very stern disciplinarian.

"Today," he intoned in a booming voice, "I want to talk to you about an environmental disaster in the ocean. There is a virtual island of garbage, hideous plastics, various forms of debris in the Pacific."

"And island of garbage?" Denique uttered out loud. "I never heard of such a thing!" To herself, she thought, "This tall old man must be crazy."

Mr. Buckingham looked right at Denique. "Miss—" he consulted his records and found the name of the new student— "Miss Giles, are you accustomed to talking out in class while the teacher is speaking? Or do you think you perhaps have more to offer your seatmate than I do?"

Jaris glanced back. He recognized the girl. He shuddered.

"I just said I never heard of that," Denique replied. "I *whispered*." Her voice was indignant. She felt that Mr. Buckingham had no right to humiliate her.

"No whispering or talking of any kind is permitted in this class unless you have been recognized to speak," Mr. Buckingham commanded. "As for this dreadful mess of garbage in the ocean, I am not surprised you know nothing about it. Many in your generation know nothing except what is on Facebook or something tweeted about the inane lives of worthless celebrities."

Mr. Buckingham then went into detail about the problems in the ocean. "We are thoughtlessly dumping every form of waste—solid, liquid, and gas—into the ocean. We are treating this priceless resource as a dump. We cannot yet imagine what effect this will have on marine life, on the earth itself."

After class, as the students filed out of the room, Jaris saw Kevin in the hallway and spoke to him in a whisper. "I'm gonna apologize to her for laughing about the shorts thing. I feel bad about it."

"You're crazy," Kevin responded. "She's a mean little twit."

"No," Jaris insisted, "I acted bad. I need to apologize."

14

Jaris walked over to where Denique and Alonee were standing together.

Jaris looked right at Denique and apologized. "Hey, I'm sorry about this morning. I was out of line laughing like that." Jaris remembered Oliver saying the girl's name was Denique, and he said, "I'm sorry, Denique."

"I bet you are," Denique snapped. "You had second thoughts 'cause you think maybe now you can come on to me. You think I'm the new chick, so maybe I'm available. Well, forget it, dude. I got your number. You're everything I hate about guys and then some."

"Whoa!" Jaris exclaimed, stunned.

"I told you, fool," Kevin crowed from a few feet away.

"Denique," Alonee advised, "Jaris is sincerely apologizing. Don't blow him off like that."

"Is he your boyfriend, Alonee?" Denique asked.

"No, but he's a very dear friend," Alonee explained. "We've known each other since we were little kids, and he's a really good guy."

"Well, as far as I'm concerned, he can go fly a kite," Denique sneered.

Alonee and Denique walked away together, while Denique continued griping. "That Buckingham is an old fool. He's like a dictator. I'll never learn anything in that class. How can you learn anything when some jerk is terrorizing the class like he does?"

"You'll get used to him," Alonee told her. "He really cut me down to size once when I was talking in class, but I like him anyway."

"And that idiot who teaches English, Langston Myers!" Denique fumed. "All those asides about the book he wrote. Who cares if he wrote a book?"

"Denique, look," Alonee said firmly, "no offense, but you need to work on that attitude. You won't be happy at all at Tubman—or anywhere—if you keep on being so negative."

"Oh, don't worry, I'll *never* be happy here," Denique declared. "I know that. Before my father pulled the rug out from under our family, Mom took me and my sister to the academy where we were going. The teachers there were all so wonderful. They were smart and friendly. I would have been so happy there." Denique spoke with both anger and sadness.

"You know, Denique," Alonee told her, "that boy who loaned you his sweater, Trevor Jenkins? Let me tell you something about that family. Trevor has three brothers, and they were all just toddlers when their dad left. Their mother is a nurse's aide, and she raised those four boys all by herself. She worked ten, twelve hours a day in a hard, dirty job, just to feed and clothe and house her sons. The oldest two boys are in the army now, and Trevor's brother is in college. It's such a good family."

Alonee glanced at Denique to see whether she was getting through to her.

Denique was reading a text from someone. Alonee decided to keep trying.

"Yet you should see how they live in that little old house. They've made the best of a horrible situation. You've got to look at the bad stuff that happens to you as a challenge, Denique. I know you're disappointed you couldn't go to that school you liked so much. But you can learn a lot here at Tubman, and you can make friends."

"You don't understand," Denique cried, her eyes filling with tears. She hadn't been checking a text; she had been feeling sorry for herself. "Maybe that Trevor guy can make the best of it 'cause he never had anything good. But I had a great life. I had this beautiful room where I could bring my friends. I had my own laptop and my iPhone, and now I don't have anything. Our house was foreclosed when Mom couldn't pay the mortgage, and they took everything, even the furniture. It's so not fair."

Denique's face wrinkled in disgust. "Alonee. I know what you're trying to do.

You think you can make me feel better by telling me stuff like that, but it doesn't help. We've been brought down so bad, me and my family. *It's not fair*. We don't deserve this. Mom was a good wife and mother—"

"Denique, a father can't just quit on his family like that," Alonee advised. "He has to pay something in child support. It's the law."

"Oh, he quit his engineer job," Denique said, grimacing. "Now he's spooning off his parents. Mom took him to court, and his lawyer said he was penniless. No job, no nothing. Mom was a homemaker all those years, so she didn't have any skills to get a good job that paid well. She's got this crummy little office job where she makes chump change. My dad got us good, Alonee. I just hate him so much it gives me a headache thinking about him."

"Denique," Alonee ordered, "listen to me. I'm so sorry such a bad thing happened in your life, but you're pretty and healthy and smart. We're young, Denique. We can make good lives for ourselves, no matter what's happened. Don't let this stuff ruin your life. When you hate like that, Denique, you don't hurt the person you hate. You hurt yourself."

Denique stopped, turned, and looked right at Alonee. "I hear what you're saying, but like what happened this morning. It was like, is this the way it's gonna be? I'm down, and I'm screwed. It's like the whole world is laughing at me and my family 'cause we've lost it all."

Alonee didn't know what more to say. The two girls walked on to their next class.

CHAPTER TWO

Athena Edson and Chelsea Spain, Jaris Spain's fourteen-year-old sister were in their first class of the day. They were waiting for the teacher. They were both new freshmen at Tubman High. Athena nudged her friend.

"Chelsea, look," she whispered. "That girl just came to Tubman last week. Her name's Lindall Giles. She's kinda pretty, isn't she?"

Lindall sat in the last row of the classroom, staring directly into her book. She had big dark eyes. She reminded Chelsea of a scared little chipmunk. "She seems shy," Chelsea whispered.

"Uh-huh," Athena agreed. "Let's invite her to join us under the pepper trees for lunch. I bet she'd like that. We can always use more people in our gang." The girls and some other kids usually had lunch together under the pepper trees on campus.

"Yeah!" Chelsea said. That was one of the things Chelsea loved about Athena. She was wild sometimes, but she had a big heart.

The teacher entered the room, and the class began.

Just before lunch that day, Athena caught up with Lindall. "Hi," Athena greeted. "I'm Athena Edson, and this is my friend, Chelsea Spain. What's your name?"

The girl looked nervous. "Lindall Giles," she answered in a small voice. She looked down at the tops of her shoes instead of at the two girls in front of her.

"Lindall," Chelsea said, "we always eat lunch over there under the pepper trees. You look like a nice girl. Wanna join us?"

"I don't know," Lindall murmured. She carried an old backpack.

"You bring lunch?" Athena asked. "Sometimes one of us forgets to bring lunch. Then we share."

"Uh … yeah," Lindall replied. Her eyes darted back and forth as though she wanted to escape.

"Whatcha got for lunch?" Chelsea asked. "My pop packed my lunch. We had turkey last night, and he made sandwiches. Pop makes the best sandwiches of anybody on earth. He puts on mayo with olive oil and pickles and some olives and tomato."

Athena made a face. "That is all so fattening," she remarked. "I've got low-fat yogurt and apple slices."

"Come on, Lindall," Chelsea urged, "let's go to lunch."

They all walked toward the pepper trees. Lindall looked terrified. She seemed to be going along only because she was afraid to say no. Lindall had always had trouble dealing with people, even other kids. She was supposed to be at that academy with girls she knew. The headmistress there had assured Lindall's mother that the shy little girl would slowly be brought out of her shell. The teachers would be looking out for her.

When Lindall saw Keisha and Falisha under the pepper trees, she looked even more frightened. This was all happening too fast.

"I … I better go," Lindall mumbled.

"Why?" Chelsea asked. Chelsea introduced Keisha and Falisha, but Lindall said nothing. Chelsea asked, "You got something to drink with your lunch? I got a couple of little bottles of orange juice. You can have one."

"Uh, Mom forgot to pack my lunch," Lindall stammered.

"That's okay," Athena told her. "My mom *always* forgets to pack my lunch."

"Here," Chelsea offered, thrusting one of her turkey sandwiches at Lindall. "My pop made two sandwiches, and I can only eat one."

Lindall looked at the sandwich as if *it* would bite her. But then she took it, and began nibbling at it. She washed it down with an orange juice from Chelsea.

"Where'd you go to school before, Lindall?" Keisha asked.

"Private school," Lindall answered. She thought the turkey sandwich was the best thing she'd eaten in a long time. Since her family got poor, she ate a lot of beans and rice.

"Boys and girls?" Falisha asked.

"No, just girls," Lindall replied.

"Ewww!" Athena exclaimed. "Bummer. Major bummer. I'd freak."

Chelsea giggled. "Me too!"

"I think it would be nice to go to an all-girls school," remarked Inessa Weaver. Inessa was another friend who'd just arrived under the pepper trees. She was a very cautious girl who didn't like a lot of people, including poor people and noisy boys. "Boys are a bother. Maurice Moore deliberately put his dirty old wad of gum on my seat in math. Luckily, I saw it before I sat down.'"

All the girls laughed. Lindall stared at them in wonderment. The girls seemed so relaxed and happy together. She wanted to be like that. She longed to be like that, but it was hard for her.

"Know what?" Chelsea stated in a confidential voice. "Something so amazing happened to me. Remember, whatever we say stays here, so don't tell anybody else."

"What happened, Chel?" Athena demanded. "Tell us, girl."

"I bet it's about a boy," Inessa sniffed.

"You guys," Chelsea began, "me and Heston were walking home together, and there was a real pretty sky." Chelsea was leaning forward and speaking softly. "It was getting dark, and it was like a magical time of day. We were holding hands while we walked, and all of a sudden he kissed me!"

"Ugh! A sloppy old boy kiss," Inessa sneered, making a face.

"No!" Chelsea protested. "It was so nice. It was so sweet. It was like a butterfly

26

landed on my lips for just a second and then flew away. I got goose bumps all over."

"Wow!" Athena remarked. "A guy kissed me the other day, and it was horrible. He was older. It was awful. It hurt. His lips kinda stuck to mine, and I got sick. I pushed him away. He's a junior, and I'm never gonna see him again."

"Weren't your parents mad that you were letting a junior boy kiss you?" Keisha asked.

"They didn't know," Athena explained. "They never know anything." Athena turned to Chelsea. "It was that dude I met at the twenty-four-seven store. Vic Stevens. Your father gave him a hard time when he found him at our house. Remember, the time your dad was bringing back my phone? Your father was real mean to Vic and I was kinda glad."

Athena paused a moment. She seemed to thinking about something.

"You know what, Chel?" she asked. "It's so weird. Sometimes I think *your*

27

father worries about me more than my own father does."

Lindall listened to it all with a sense of fascination. Finally, she announced, "My sister and I go to private schools with just girls. I mean we did. But then the money ran out." She finished her sandwich.

The other girls looked at each other. Hadn't Lindall just said that?

"Did you like the sandwich, Lindall?" Chelsea asked.

"Yes, thanks. It was awfully good," Lindall responded.

"My pop is the best cook ever," Chelsea declared.

"Is that what he does?" Lindall asked.

"No, he owns his own garage—Spain's Auto Care," Chelsea replied. "He's a good mechanic too. He's proud of that. He calls all the old cars he fixes 'beaters.' Does your father cook, Lindall?"

"No," the girl said curtly. She looked in-describably sad. The other girls noticed. No one said anything, except for Inessa, who was not as sensitive as the others. "What *does* your father do, Lindall?" she asked.

"Engineer," Lindall answered.

"Oh, that's cool," Athena said. "He must make a lot of money."

Falisha hadn't said much until now. Her father had had a drinking problem and had abused her mother. Falisha's mother—Ms. Colbert, who taught science at Tubman—left him years ago. Falisha didn't even remember her father, even though he sometimes sent her birthday cards. Falisha loved her mother a lot.

"My mom is Ms. Colbert, the science teacher," Falisha told Lindall. "My parents haven't been together for a long time. But I'm getting a stepfather pretty soon. His name is Shadrach. He was in the Iraq War. He lost an eye and was really badly scarred by an explosion. Now he runs a rescue shelter for opossum. When people first see him, his scars make him look scary. But he's so friendly and nice that everybody soon stops seeing his scars. I didn't like him at first

29

'cause he has some scars, but now I sorta like him a lot. He makes Mom laugh, and sometimes he makes me laugh too."

Lindall licked her dry lips nervously. Then she spoke in a soft voice that hardly anybody could hear. They had to lean close to hear her words.

"My father is gone," Lindall confessed.

"Gone?" Inessa repeated. "You mean dead?"

"No, he moved away from us," Lindall replied. "He didn't like us anymore."

Chelsea felt terrible. A father turning against his family was an incredibly awful thing. Lindall could have just as well said aliens abducted her father. Chelsea would have had just as hard a time understanding. Fathers just didn't do that. Chelsea knew a lot of kids at Tubman whose parents were divorced. But usually both parents continued to love and see their children.

"That's a sad thing, Lindall," Chelsea sympathized.

Chelsea had a dessert in her tote bag. Pop made some amazing chocolate chip cookies. They had more bits of chewy chocolate than you got in the store-bought cookies. Chelsea always added a couple chocolate chip cookies to her tote bag in case she got hungry. And, after eating her lunch, she seemed always to have room for a chocolate chip cookie. Normally, Chelsea just gobbled down the store-bought kind. But Pop's chocolate chip cookies were so good that she had a ritual about eating them. She nibbled slowly around the edges, working her way into the center. The center was the yummiest and gooiest part of the whole cookie.

"Lindall," Chelsea offered, "my pop makes the best chocolate chip cookies, and I got an extra one in my bag. Here, try it." Chelsea pulled out the cookie, which was lovingly wrapped in a little plastic baggie. She handed it to Lindall, who took it rather quickly.

"Thanks, Chelsea," Lindall said. "It looks really good." She tasted it, and then

31

she smiled. "It tastes even better than it looks."

It was almost time for afternoon classes. The girls gathered their things for the climb up the trail to the walkway. As they walked, Chelsea drew up alongside Lindall.

"Lindall," Chelsea told her, "when you've been here at Tubman for a while, you'll like it. Mosta the kids are nice, and the teachers are pretty good too. It's gonna be way better than the all-girl school you were going to go to. Boys can be awful sometimes. But it's much funner when boys are going to school with you. They do dumb things, and they make you laugh. And they do nice things, and they give you goose bumps. It would be pretty dull if there weren't any boys."

Athena chimed in. "Chelsea's right, Lindall. I like all my girlfriends, but I couldn't stand it if there weren't boys around. Even when they're being bad, boys are really exciting, I think."

"Yeah," Inessa agreed. "If there weren't any boys around, who would stick gum on my chair? I mean, who'd grab my math book and run with it, just to be funny?"

The girls laughed. Even Lindall chuckled a little. It was the first time Chelsea had seen her smile.

Lindall and Chelsea both had world history together, and they broke off from the others. As they walked, Chelsea asked, "You got any brothers or sisters, Lindall?"

"I got a sister. She's older than me," Lindall answered. "She's a senior here. In our old house, we had our separate bedrooms. But now we gotta share a bedroom, and sometimes I guess I bother her."

"Is she nice?" Chelsea asked.

"Sometimes, I guess. Sometimes she's not. You got a sister, Chelsea?" Lindall asked.

"No, I got a big brother," Chelsea told her. "He's a senior too. He's real bossy sometimes. He tries to tell me what I can do and what I can't do. Sometimes he chases my boyfriends and stuff, and he even spies on me to make sure I'm okay."

"I bet you get mad at him, huh?" Lindall asked.

"Yeah, sometimes," Chelsea admitted. "But I love him a lot too. I could smack him sometimes when he bosses me around about what clothes I should buy. But he's pretty wonderful most of the time. I'm so glad he's my brother. His name is Jaris, and he's always looking out for me. Even when he's, you know, bugging me, I know it's 'cause he loves me. He's a lot like my pop."

Lindall looked a little sad when Chelsea mentioned her father, and Chelsea was sorry she said it. She'd probably reminded Lindall of her own father who'd gone away.

Chelsea planned to take a trip to the mall after school to buy some clothes. She had some gift money from her Grandma Jessie, and she was eager to spend it. Grandma Jessie had wanted Chelsea to go to a ritzy boarding school instead of to Tubman. But that was never going to happen if

Chelsea could help it. So her grandmother sent Chelsea a nice money gift. In her note with the gift, Grandma Jessie explained the reason for it. She said that, if Chelsea was going to such a poor school, she might at least wear nice clothes. Chelsea had no problem with being told to buy new clothes.

But Chelsea loved Tubman High School too much to go anywhere else. All her friends were there, and Jaris was there. Never in a million years would she want to go to a ritzy boarding school. Her parents wouldn't have wanted her to go either because they would have missed her too much.

So, even though Chelsea resented Grandma Jessie trying to get her out of Tubman, she did appreciate the money. She sat right down and wrote her grandmother a very nice thank-you letter. Mom insisted on that anyway. Chelsea wanted to text Grandma the thank-you, but Grandma would want a handwritten note in the mail. She had been a real estate agent before she retired, and now she wanted nothing to do with text messages or e-mails.

Chelsea could have taken the bus to the mall, but Jaris offered to drive her and any of her friends who wanted to go. So, after the last class, Chelsea, Athena, and Keisha piled into Jaris's Honda, and they all took off for a shopping spree.

"We met a new girl in school today," Chelsea told Jaris. "She's real shy and kinda scared, Jaris. She used to go to a private school, and Tubman seems big to her. We asked her to eat lunch with us under the pepper trees so she'd have some friends." ⌣

"Chelsea gave her a turkey sandwich and a chocolate chip cookie 'cause it looked like she didn't have any lunch," Athena added. "She's kinda poor."

Jaris turned and smiled at his sister. "That was nice of you, chili pepper. You're all right."

Chelsea giggled, "Anyways, I think we made Lindall—that's her name—feel better.

She was kinda laughing at our jokes at the end of the lunch."

"Yeah," Keisha said. "She was like a little lost puppy at first, but she warmed up."

"We met a new girl in the senior class today too," Jaris responded. "Me and Trevor and Kevin. Not such a happy experience." Jaris chuckled, remembering the tear in Denique's shorts.

"What happened, Jaris?" Chelsea demanded, seeing the look of mischief in her brother's eyes.

"Oh, well, it was kinda windy today, you know," Jaris explained. "Me and Trevor and Kevin were walking behind this girl, and a gust of wind took her papers. She stooped to get them, and she was wearing these tight shorts. Well, they split, and we saw her red panties." Jaris laughed again.

All three girls started laughing too.

"What'd the girl do when you started laughing?" Chelsea asked.

"I bet she was mad," Athena guessed.

" 'Mad' isn't the word for it," Jaris said. "She wanted to kill us, I think, especially me and Kevin. Poor Trevor loaned her his sweater to, you know, cover her backside. So she gave him a pass. But, oh boy, this chick hates me and Kevin big time."

They were in the mall parking lot by now, and the girls' attention turned to their shopping mission.

CHAPTER THREE

That night, Trevor Jenkins worked his shift at the Chicken Shack. He liked the beautiful girl Jaris had hired, Amberlynn Parson. But she had already turned down Trevor's bids for a date. He had had high hopes to date her, but now she clearly wasn't the least bit interested in him. Few girls were. Trevor felt lonelier than ever.

Trevor had also found out that Amberlynn was really interested in Jaris, who had a girlfriend, Sereeta Prince. Jaris had loved Sereeta since middle school, though they only got close during their junior year at Tubman High School. Trevor felt that he and Amberlynn were in the same boat. Trevor liked Amberlynn, but she didn't like him. Amberlynn liked Jaris. But he was so much in love with Sereeta that he barely looked at other girls.

One of the other workers at the Chicken Shack was Jenny, who was married. Jenny watched Trevor glancing at Amberlynn during his shift. Jenny thought that if she wasn't married, she might be interested in dating Trevor. He was a nice guy. Jenny thought, "How sad. The ones we want don't want us. The ones who want us, we don't like."

Jenny even told Neal, the Chicken Shack boss, about how lonely Trevor was. "The poor guy," Neal responded. "He'd really like to go out with Amberlynn, but he's totally not her type. I wish I knew some nice girl for Trevor, but I just don't."

Trevor drove Amberlynn home once or twice, trying for a date. But he didn't do that anymore. It hurt too much to look over and see her lovely profile and to yearn for one date—one measly date. He wondered why she couldn't just give him that. What harm would it do her? She might find out that she enjoyed being with him. She wouldn't even give Trevor a chance.

When Trevor got home from work, his brother Tommy was getting ready for a night out with his girlfriend. Tommy was in the community college, and he never lacked for chicks. He was much cooler than Trevor. "You know what, Tommy," Trevor announced, "I'm gonna just stop thinkin' about it." Trevor sat down on Tommy's bed.

"Thinking about what, little brother?" Tommy asked as he splashed aftershave lotion on his face.

"Chicks," Trevor replied. "I'm done with them. They're not worth it, man. I'm gonna just forget about them. When I see a cute chick, I'm gonna just walk on by and think about something else, like football. I don't need 'em. They're just a pain anyway. At lunchtime at Tubman, I'm not goin' down to eat with my friends under the eucalyptus trees either. Jaris cuddlin' with Sereeta ... Kevin with his head in Carissa's lap ... Alonee Lennox and Oliver Randall gigglin' with each other. It makes me sick to watch."

Trevor lay back on the bed, his head on the pillow. "I hate the whole scene. I'm done with all that. I'm gonna eat my lunch on one of the benches behind the gym. I can get some homework done too. Everybody's always yakking down there under the trees. Yeah ... it's like a big load off my mind. It's over." Trevor took a deep breath and then said, "Actually, I hate chicks, and that's the truth, man."

"Come on, bro," Tommy responded. "You're just goin' through a bad patch."

"No, I mean it," Trevor said. "I loved Vanessa Allen a lot, and she just wanted to use me in her crooked schemes. She never cared about me. No chick's ever cared about me. Amberlynn, down at the Chicken Shack, she looks at me like I'm a cockroach. Well, I don't need her. I don't need no chicks."

"Hey, Trevor, I could fix you up with a girl if you wanted," Tommy suggested as he leaned with one hand on his dresser. "Liza, a babe I know, she's got a younger sister who—"

"No, thanks," Trevor almost shouted. "I don't want some pity date. I don't want my brother scrounging up some chick. I don't want nobody goin' out with me just to do me a favor. You did that once before, Tommy, and I hated it. 'Here, babe, do me a good turn and go out with my loser brother. The poor dude can't get any action on his own.' No thanks. I'm sick of it all. If I wanna go to the movies, I'll go alone. I don't mind goin' places alone."

Trevor stormed out of the room and left the house, slamming the door behind him. In a few minutes, Tommy drove off in his car to pick up his date.

Outside, Trevor saw no moon in the sky. The night was totally dark, like Trevor's mood. Behind the Jenkins's small house were fields and few rundown houses.

Beyond that was Grant Street, where the apartments were, the projects. The government paid part of the rent for the welfare people who lived in some of the units. Others were scraping by on low-paying jobs. The gangbangers hung out on Grant. It was the worst part of the neighborhood.

Trevor crossed the fields and got on Grant. Hip-hop flowed out of some of the apartments. It was dangerous walking around there at night, but Trevor didn't care. If Ma knew Trevor was walking these mean streets late at night, she'd have a fit.

Mickey Jenkins—Ma—worried about Trevor, her youngest son. Her husband had left when her four boys were little more than babies. She'd raised three of them already to be good men. Two were in the U.S. Army, and Tommy was in the community college. But she worried about Trevor. He seemed the most vulnerable of the four, the one most likely to get into trouble. She'd always told her boys she'd rather have a dead son than one in prison.

But right now, Trevor didn't much care which way he ended up. He walked down the street, swinging his shoulders and snapping his fingers. He was listening to the beat of a violent rap song coming from a parked car somewhere.

The bus stopped on the corner of the street, and a woman got off—just the one woman. She was about thirty-five, and she wore a pale green pants suit. She looked like she probably worked in an office downtown. She probably had a crummy job making chump change. Otherwise, she wouldn't be coming home to Grant Street. Only losers lived on Grant.

The woman frequently looked behind her as she walked. She walked fast. She apparently was not used to being in a bad neighborhood. Trevor wondered what a nicely dressed, good-looking woman was doing here anyway. This was where the Nite Ryders hung out. No woman, especially not a pretty one, should be walking on Grant at this hour.

Trevor saw two men in the shadows just beyond where the woman would soon pass. They looked like gangbangers. Would they try to steal the woman's purse? She carried a nice shoulder bag, clutching it tightly. If they grabbed for her purse, they'd probably knock her down. If she fought for it—and she might—who knows what they would do to her? A few weeks ago, an older woman fought for her purse and ended up with a broken hip.

"Ah, none of my business," Trevor thought.

Trevor shuddered. The blood from the last murder on Grant still stained the sidewalk. Trevor kept telling himself it was none of his business. "Her problem, not mine," he told himself.

The woman was already close to the place where the two men lurked. Trevor would have to hurry if he was going to catch up with her. Before he realized it, he was walking on the sidewalk behind the woman in the pale green pants suit.

"Ma'am, excuse me," Trevor called out.

She turned, terror in her eyes. She was very pretty, even prettier than she looked from a distance.

"Ma'am, don't be scared," Trevor assured her. "It's okay. I'm a senior at Tubman High School, and I saw you walkin' here all alone. I was worried about you. So, if you don't mind, I'll just tag along with you till you get home."

The terror faded a little from her eyes. "I'm coming home from work," she responded, clutching her purse. "I had to work late. I'm really scared to be walking down this street at this hour. But I don't have a car. Thank you so much, young man." Her voice was shaky.

Trevor noticed that the two men in the shadows slipped away when Trevor came along.

"Where do you live, ma'am?" Trevor asked.

"That apartment building at the end of the street," she replied.

"Okay, I'll walk you to your door," Trevor said. "Y'know, it's probably better if you tell your boss you can't work late if it means coming home like this in the dark."

"I need the job so badly," the woman explained. "Jobs aren't so easy to come by these days. I have kids to support."

"You work downtown, huh?" Trevor asked.

"Yes," she answered.

"You might be better off taking the fifty-six bus, ma'am," Trevor suggested. "It'll let you off by the deli there. There's a bright streetlight, and you won't have the long walk down Grant. That'd be safer. The fifty-nine bus gives you a much longer and more dangerous walk."

She smiled. "Thank you so much. That's an excellent tip. I have been taking the fifty-nine because I didn't know about the other one. What did you say your name was?"

"My name is Trevor Jenkins," he replied.

"And you said you go to Tubman High?" she asked.

"Yes, ma'am," Trevor said.

"My girls go there too," the woman told him. "Thanks so much, Trevor. You're a fine young man."

Trevor saw her safely into her apartment. Then he turned and jogged home.

When he got home, he saw Tommy's Cavalier in the yard.

"Hey, dude, where ya been?" Tommy yelled.

"Just jogging. What're you doin' home, man?" Trevor asked. "I thought you had a date with Liza."

A pretty girl climbed out of the car and gave Trevor a big smile. "I'm Shalonda Reeves, baby," she announced. "Oh, you're a big handsome one. You're a good lookin' sucka." Liza looked out the passenger side of the car and smiled too.

Shalonda walked over to where Trevor stood and put her hands on his chest. "Say, big boy, you're built," she remarked.

Trevor felt like strangling his brother. He told him not to do this. Shalonda Reeves was doing Tommy a favor. The whole deal made Trevor feel like two cents. If Trevor had asked this girl out, she would have laughed in his face. But now, as a favor to the big stud Tommy, she would be sweet to poor loser Trevor, at least for the night.

"Let's go, Trev," Tommy urged.

"I can't go anywhere," Trevor objected. "I got stuff to do for school."

"Come on, dude. That can wait," Tommy told him.

Shalonda ran her soft hand along Trevor's cheek. "Come on, babe. We're goin' to a club. You're hot, Trevor. I wanna be with you."

Trevor felt as though he'd like to scream, but that wouldn't be fair to the girl. She was just doing Tommy a favor.

"Look, Shalonda," Trevor said as calmly as he could, "you're a hot chick, and I really appreciate the invitation. But I just can't go with you guys. I just can't."

50

Shalonda looked at Tommy, who shrugged. "Ah, c'mon," Tommy suggested. "We can have some fun without him. See ya later, Trev."

As the car pulled away, Trevor felt so done with chicks.

CHAPTER FOUR

Denique Giles and Marko Lane met in a doorway going to English.

"Get out of my way, jerk," Denique snarled.

"Hey, babe," Marko reacted, "all I done was say you were a hot chick, that's all. What're you takin' offense at that? What's wrong with you?" Jasmine Benson, his girlfriend, was nowhere in sight, and Marko liked Denique's curves. To Marko, most of the chicks at Tubman, including Jasmine, seemed too skinny. But this girl had curves. Marko loved Jasmine, but sometimes he got bored. Denique was a shot of jalapeño pepper, and Marko enjoyed hot stuff.

"Just drop dead," Denique snarled. "Would you do that for me?"

Marko Lane had to get going to his class, so he disappeared. He used to be in Langston Myers's English class, the class Denique was in, until he ran afoul of the teacher. Now he was transferred to another English class.

Denique Giles walked into Mr. Myers's class. She was glad on the days the class was scheduled in the morning. The sooner she was done with the class, the better. She didn't like Mr. Myers, nor did she like the bombastic science teacher, Mr. Buckingham. But she did like Ms. Torie McDowell, who taught the history and political science classes. Just about everybody at Tubman liked Ms. McDowell. She was exciting, fair, and fun to listen to, and Denique was taking a world history class from Ms. McDowell. Denique was surprised that someone as good as Ms. McDowell was even a teacher at this inferior school.

"Today we are going to talk about allusion," Mr. Myers began, "a fascinating topic. Who has read the chapter I assigned and can give me a brief description of allusion?"

Jaris raised his hand. "It's a way of suggesting more than what appears on the page. For example, a line of poetry may allude to some past historic event."

Denique stared at Jaris Spain. That was the rude lout who laughed at her when she bent over and split her shorts. She couldn't believe that he was making an intelligent comment about anything. He was quite handsome too, but she refused to concede that. All she could think of was how he and his friend, somebody called Kevin Walker, howled at her misfortune.

"Yes," Mr. Myers replied. "Let us examine this poem by Wilfred Owen, 'The Parable of the Old Man and the Young.' Who can tell us something about this poet?"

"He was in World War I," Sereeta Prince answered. "He died in battle when he was only twenty-five."

"Yes," Mr. Myers replied. "This poem is actually about young men dying in wars because old men will not listen to reason. How is that an allusion to something else?"

Jaris raised his hand again. "Well, it alludes to Abraham in the Bible. He was about to sacrifice his only son, but then an angel told him not to. He listened to the angel and spared his son."

"Indeed," Mr. Myers said. "How do the final four lines complete the point of the poem?"

Oliver Randall spoke up. "Well, Abraham held back from killing his son. But the nations of Europe would not hold back from sacrificing a whole generation of young men in a senseless conflict. The nations of Europe were not as wise as Abraham in listening to the voice of reason."

Denique looked at Oliver. He was very handsome. He was not one of the fools who had laughed at her, but he hadn't been there. Perhaps he would have if he had been there because Denique had noticed he was friends with Jaris. Denique's gaze roamed to where Kevin Walker sat. He seemed to be looking right at her, smirking. Was he reliving the delightful moment when he got to laugh at her misery? She really hated him.

Kevin Walker spoke next. "The poem ends saying that 'half the seed of Europe' died in that war."

"How intelligent those two louts, Jaris and Kevin, seem in this class," Denique thought. "And the other day, when the wind was blowing and my shorts split, they were like howling idiots. That's how men are," Denique thought bitterly. "One minute they're fine and you learn to trust them. The next minute they show their true colors."

Like her father, Denique thought. He seemed to be a good, hardworking man who loved and took care of his family. Denique loved and respected him. And then suddenly it all changed. He was packed and gone. "Men are deceivers," Denique thought. "You can't trust them."

There was no warning before Mr. Giles left. He seemed a little preoccupied in the weeks before he left, but Denique thought he was just working too hard. Nobody expected what happened. He left just a terse note, "I'm sorry, sorry," and departed.

Denique took good notes in class. She wanted to graduate high school and get a job. She'd wanted to go to college, but that was now out of the question. Denique, Lindall, and their mother lived in that horrible little apartment over on Grant. Gangbangers tagged everything. Denique had to get a job as soon as possible after high school. With her and her mother bringing in money, the family could move to a better, safer place. Denique felt she owed that to her poor mother.

Denique watched Jaris, Kevin, and Oliver walk from class. They were, all three of them, as thick as thieves. Denique thought that that proved Oliver was no good either, even though he seemed more civilized.

Jaris—fool that he was—had at least made a feeble stab at apologizing for laughing at her, Denique recalled. Kevin Walker didn't even do that much. He was the worst of the lot. He seemed like a total freak.

Then Denique noticed another boy join Jaris, Kevin, and Oliver. They all joined in animated conversation. He was the boy who loaned her his sweater to cover her torn shorts. The others just ogled her red panties. He hadn't laughed at her, and he was kind enough to help her. Trevor Jenkins. Yes, that was his name. But how could he hang with idiots like Jaris and Kevin?

Denique spotted Alonee, and she walked over to her. "Alonee, that guy Trevor Jenkins. Is he really friends with Jaris Spain and that Kevin creep?" she asked.

"Yes, Denique, and they're all nice guys," Alonee replied. "So Jaris and Kevin made a mistake laughing at you. Can't you just forget it?"

Denique remembered something else. Last night, when her mother came home from work, she told Denique and Lindall about a senior from Tubman High School. He had been so worried about her walking down Grant that he escorted her home. Denique's mother hadn't mentioned the boy's name. Now Denique wondered who the boy was.

Denique told Alonee what had happened with her mother last night. Denique knew that her mother would be on break at her office now so she could make a quick call.

"Mom," Denique asked, "remember you telling me about the guy last night who said he was a senior at Tubman, the one who walked you home? Did he tell you his name, Mom?" A strange look came over Denique's face. "Thanks, Mom," she said, ending the call.

Denique looked at Alonee. "It was that guy Trevor Jenkins, Alonee. Can you believe it?"

"Yeah, I can," Alonee responded. "Trevor's like that. He has a very good heart. They all do, Denique. Really they do. None of those boys would refuse to help someone if they could. Trevor lives close to Grant, and he jogs around there. He must have seen your mom going down that dark street and worried about her."

Denique watched the four boys walk away across the campus—Jaris, Kevin, Oliver, and Trevor. She still couldn't believe Trevor Jenkins wanted to be with those jerks. Denique wanted to see Trevor and thank him for helping her mother last night. But she wasn't going to approach those three jerks and give them a chance for another laugh. She had to get Trevor alone.

Denique waited for her chance. At lunchtime, she saw Jaris, Kevin, and Oliver head down a little trail to a grove of eucalyptus trees. She wondered whether Trevor would follow. She was hoping he wouldn't.

Trevor walked slowly to the vending machines. He bought himself a ham and cheese sandwich and a soda. Then he walked to a bench behind the gym, out of sight from Denique. The place was one of the most out-of-the-way spots on campus. Nobody was around, and Trevor sat down.

Denique had a peanut butter and jelly sandwich that she had made for herself last night. She walked slowly toward where Trevor had gone behind the gym. She figured he was sitting on one of those secluded benches.

"Hi," Denique hailed, rounding the corner of the gym.

Trevor looked up. "Hi," he responded, continuing to eat his sandwich. The sandwich was pretty good, much better than the tuna fish sandwiches his mother used to make for him.

"Mom told me what you did," Denique remarked.

"Huh?" Trevor looked worried. "What did I do? I don't think I even know your mother. I don't even know you, girl, except I loaned you my sweater yesterday. What's goin' on?"

"We live on those dirty, ratty apartments on Grant Street," Denique explained. "Last night, Mom was walking home from the bus. You were worried about her walking alone on the dark street, and you walked with her. That was pretty cool, and I know she thanked you. But I want to thank you too."

Denique sat down on the bench with Trevor, but all the way at the other end. She didn't want him to get any ideas.

"Oh yeah?" Trevor replied with a grin. "That was your mom? I'll be darned. What a coincidence. Well, you know, I was over there last night, and I seen her walking from the bus. I saw these two guys too in the darkness. I got a little worried they'd rip off her purse or something. That's why I got mixed up in it. Your mom, she's a real pretty lady. Nice too. I'm glad I could help her."

"All the guys here at Tubman seem like freakin' fools, Trevor," Denique commented. "But you're all right. Thanks again for helping my mom. I guess I already thanked you for lending me your sweater."

Denique didn't know what more to say. Then she realized she'd forgotten her manners.

"Oh," she said, "I'm Denique Giles, in case you didn't know. I sorta hate guys, Trevor, but, like I said, you're all right."

"Well," Trevor answered, "I pretty much hate chicks, Denique. I got nothin' but grief from them, so I sorta swore off 'em, if you know what I'm sayin'."

Denique looked hard at Trevor. "No kidding?" she asked.

"I wouldn't kid ya," Trevor asserted.

"Mom tells me that having hate in you makes you sick, Trevor," Denique commented. "But I can't help myself."

"Me neither," Trevor responded.

"Mom tells me hating just makes a person miserable," Denique went on.

"I guess that's so," Trevor agreed, " 'cause I sure feel miserable."

Denique gave Trevor a grudging smile. "If I wasn't so messed up in my head, I'd sorta like you, Trevor," she confessed. "But it would just end up bad anyway."

"Yeah," Trevor said. "It always does. So we better just leave it alone. I guess there are a lot worse things than being lonely. There's being with people who end up hurting you. That's the worst. You try to trust somebody and, you know, love them. Then you find out they aren't decent people and they just trashed your love."

"Isn't that the truth!" Denique agreed, thinking about her father.

She wondered who Trevor was thinking about.

At about the same time, Chelsea and Athena were heading for their lunch spot under the pepper trees. Chelsea announced, "I'm having a sleepover, Athena, and I hope you can come."

"Yeah!" Athena exclaimed. "Who else is coming?"

"Inessa can't, but Keisha is coming," Chelsea answered. "Falisha can't, but I'm gonna ask Lindall. Okay?"

"Yeah, sure," Athena replied.

When Lindall came to eat lunch with them, Chelsea asked her, "You ever been to a sleepover, Lindall?"

"Yeah," Lindall answered. "We had this big house, and I had a beautiful big bedroom. And all my friends would come, and it was so fun. But now—"

"Well, I'm having a sleepover at my house, Lindall," Chelsea told her. "And I hope you can come."

"Yeah," Lindall responded, brightening. "If my mom says it's okay."

"It's Friday night," Chelsea said. "My pop will pick us up after school. We'll get you back home Saturday. Oh, Lindall, we'll have lots of fun. We can listen to music and watch movies, and Pop is making one of his great meals. My pop's the best cook ever. I don't know what he's making, but it'll be awesome."

Lindall smiled and remarked, "That'll be nice. I miss sleepovers. Now all my friends are on the other side of town, so I can't have them anymore."

When school was out, Chelsea and Athena walked home together. As Chelsea came into the house, Mom was working on the computer.

"Mom," Chelsea said, "Pop says it's okay if we have a sleepover Friday night. Is that okay?"

Mom looked up from her computer. She'd been working hard and looked tired. "Of course," Mom answered wearily. "Pop's the boss around here. Heaven forbid that I'd throw a monkey wrench into any plans you've worked out with your father."

"You're in a bad mood, huh, Mom?" Chelsea commented.

"No, I'm not in a bad mood," Mom snapped. She sighed and leaned back in her chair. "Actually, my principal, Mr. Maynard, is giving me more and more things to do. I sometimes think I've become the principal of the school without the pay and the honor or title."

Pop had arrived right behind Chelsea, grimy from his work at Spain's Auto Care, where he was now the owner. He'd heard Mom's comment. He stood there, transfixed. "She's complaining about old Greg Maynard! I never thought I'd live to see the day. The paragon of educational greatness, old Maynard himself, is bein' dissed by his faithful teacher, Monica Spain."

Pop was grinning from ear to ear. At one time, Pop thought his wife and Maynard were too friendly. Maynard was divorced, and he clearly liked Mom. Even Jaris and Chelsea feared that Mom admired the smooth, elegant Greg Maynard. Also, the principal seemed superior to Pop in many ways.

"He's a dear," Mom objected. "But he's piling so much of *his* work on me that I can barely do my own. If I'm going to do the principal's work, then I want the salary too."

Mom smiled weakly at Chelsea. "I'm sorry, sweetheart. I *am* in a bad mood. I'm just so tired. A sleepover would be fine. Who all is coming?"

"Athena," Chelsea began the list.

"Oh goody," Pop remarked, "my favorite little twit."

Chelsea laughed. "Then Keisha is coming, and I've invited Lindall Giles, that new girl. She's really nice, and she is real sad 'cause her father left the family. They used to have a nice place to live, and now they're over on Grant and it's bad."

"It's nice that you invited her, little girl," Pop remarked.

Jaris came through the door. "Who'd I hear you're inviting, chili pepper?" he asked.

"That new girl at school, Lindall," Chelsea answered. "Lindall Giles is her name. She doesn't have much good stuff goin' on in her life, so I wanted her to have some fun."

Jaris stood there a moment. "Uh-oh," he grunted.

"What uh-oh?" Chelsea demanded.

"That's Denique Giles's little sister," Jaris explained. "I told you about the split shorts didn't I?"

"What split shorts?" Mom asked with concern.

Chelsea started giggling.

"I'm always the last to know anything, but that's all right. I'm only the mother," Mom grumbled. "What are you talking about, Jaris. Whose shorts split?"

"Don't feel bad, babe," Pop consoled Mom. "I ain't in on this story either."

"Well," Jaris began, his voice rising to overcome Chelsea's noisy giggling. "Me and Kevin and Trevor were coming onto the campus. This girl stooped over to pick up some papers that blew off in the wind. Well … her shorts were a little too tight, and they sorta split in the back. We could see her red panties." Jaris started to chuckle. "And we laughed, me and Kevin, but Trevor didn't laugh. He gave the girl his sweater so she could cover her backside."

Pop began to laugh now. Now Jaris and Chelsea and Pop were all laughing. But Mom wasn't. Mom was glaring at her husband and her children.

"Shame on you, Jaris," Mom chided. "That was so rude to have laughed at that poor girl. *Lorenzo, stop laughing*! Imagine how embarrassed she was to begin with. Then to have some boys laughing like donkeys at her. I'm disappointed in you, Jaris."

Pop kept laughing. "Hey, like maybe this chick oughtn't wear this here size four when she's got a size fourteen backside. Y'hear what I'm sayin'? Maybe it served her right."

Another spasm of laughter erupted from Jaris and Chelsea. "She had on these bright red panties," Jaris added.

"Jaris Spain," Mom shouted, "you stop that laughing. Honestly, I thought you were more grown-up than to be acting like that."

"Were they the lacy kind?" Chelsea asked. She covered her mouth to smother her fresh spell of giggles.

When the three calmed down, Jaris continued the story.

"Anyway," Jaris explained, "this girl got really mad at Kevin and me. I tried to apologize for laughing, but she wasn't having any of that. She just yelled at me. I'm surprised her little sister is coming to your sleepover, Chelsea. I wonder if she knows—"

"Probably she doesn't know," Mom remarked. "Such an embarrassing thing as that isn't something you'd want to share with your family, poor thing."

"Yes, they were lacy," Jaris whispered to Chelsea.

Chelsea screamed in a fresh burst of giggles.

Pop chuckled.

"You're all three of you like nasty children," Mom snarled.

That night, Lindall's mother called the Spain house to thank Chelsea for the invitation to the sleepover. She said that she would be delighted to have her daughter come and that it was very sweet of Chelsea to invite her.

Pop took the call. "I'll be pickin' up Lindall and the other girls at Tubman about three thirty Friday. I'll bring her home Saturday afternoon, Mrs. Giles."

"Wonderful," Mrs. Giles responded. "I'm sure it will do Lindall so much good to be with her friends. Lindall has already told me so much about your daughter, Chelsea. She really likes her, Mr. Spain."

Jena Giles then thanked Pop again and hung up.

"Well, ain't that nice," Pop commented with genuine enthusiasm. "Chelsea feels sorry for the poor little girl who has had a lot of turmoil in her life. Now she's gonna come over and have some fun. I'll make something extra special for dinner to make it an even better visit."

Jaris drew up besides his father. "Thanks, Pop, for picking them up at school. I'd feel a little nervous doing that. I think if Denique spotted me picking up her little sister, she might attack me. This chick is really mean."

"Well," Pop remarked, "these here red panties, they maybe chafe her, especially if she's wearing these really tight pants. I mean chafing panties and tight jeans, that's enough to make a girl mean any day o' the week."

"Lorenzo," Mom growled, "why don't you shower and get into some clean clothes. While you're at it, stick your head under some cold water."

As Pop strode toward the bathroom, he grinned and winked at Chelsea and Jaris.

Later on, Chelsea was in her room, listening to hip-hop music, which she liked. Mom hated hip-hop. When Mom came into the room, Chelsea quickly turned it down. She was afraid her mother was going to scold her for listening. But Mom sat on the edge of the bed and said, "Chelsea, I'm very proud of you."

"Huh?" Chelsea responded.

"This little girl has been in school only a few days and I imagine she's frightened and lonely," Mom explained. "And you reach out to her like that and include her among your friends. Baby, I'm proud of you for making good grades and being a lovely girl. But I'm even prouder of your big heart." Mom reached out and gave Chelsea a big hug.

CHAPTER FIVE

Right after Jaris got out of classes on Friday afternoon, he got a call from Pop.

"Jaris, I'm sorry, but I got beaters lined up here bumper to bumper. And they all need to be finished by the weekend. I'm hammered, boy. You gotta pick up the girls for the sleepover," Pop told him.

Jaris's heart sank. His only hope was that Denique wouldn't be around when he picked up her sister, Lindall.

Chelsea and her friends had planned to meet Pop in the parking lot at Tubman. But Jaris texted Chelsea to meet him at his Honda. As he stood, leaning on his car, he searched the throngs of freshmen coming his way. If Jaris spotted Denique coming with her sister, he planned to duck behind the Honda. But his plan went awry. Denique was cutting through the parking lot alone on her way to a math tutorial class. She gave Jaris a dirty look and walked on. Luckily, Chelsea and her friends had not yet arrived. Jaris breathed a sigh of relief.

Chelsea, Keisha, Athena, and Lindall came then, all chattering away. Chelsea was yelling and giggling, as usual. The noise caused Denique, who was not yet out of the parking lot, to stop and turn. Denique stood still and stared as her sister climbed into the backseat of Jaris's car. Chelsea jumped into the front, and Jaris ran around the front of the car. He wanted to get out of there fast. Denique was such an angry chick; Jaris thought she would come running and drag her poor little sister out of the car. But Denique just stood there in shock. If Lindall had been boarding a spaceship, Denique could not have been more stunned.

"This is my brother, Jaris," Chelsea burbled away to Lindall. "He drives me lotsa places. He's pretty nice, 'cept when I'm shopping for clothes and he makes me buy horrible things way too big for me."

"Hi, Jaris," Lindall said. Jaris heard her whisper to Chelsea, "*He's cute!*"

"Hi, Lindall," Jaris responded cheerfully, glad that the car was in motion. He glanced in the rearview mirror. The reflection of an angry Denique Giles was growing smaller.

Jaris thought Lindall was pretty. She looked a lot like her sister, Denique, but without Denique's ugly scowl.

"Jaris's father is a real character, Lindall," Athena remarked. "You're in for a treat. This guy's something else. He gets mad at me and I get mad at him, and he yells and screams. But deep down he's a real good guy. He loves to cook, and he makes these amazing meals that nobody else makes unless they work at a fancy restaurant."

Keisha giggled. "Lindall, Athena's parents let her do anything she wants. She gets into loads of trouble, but they just laugh it off. But Chelsea's dad, he thinks Chelsea is still like nine years old or something, and she's gotta be protected."

Driving toward the Spain house, Jaris asked Lindall a question. "Lindall, has your sister talked about her experiences at Tubman?" He was fishing around to see whether Lindall knew anything about the infamous red-panty incident.

"Denique hates Tubman," Lindall answered. "She said the boys are all howling idiots. I don't know why she said that. The kids all seem okay to me, even the boys."

"Well, I guess she misses an all-girl school," Jaris remarked. "No howling idiot boys."

"Yeah," Lindall agreed.

"Do you hate Tubman too, Lindall?" Jaris asked.

"I didn't like it at first," Lindall answered. "I was scared. But Chelsea helped me a lot. Now I know a lotta nice kids. I like that Ms. Colbert in science too." Lindall took a deep breath and swallowed. "It's so fun going under the pepper trees with our group. I mean, I feel so special."

"You *are* special, Lindall," Chelsea told her. "The minute I met you, I just knew you'd be our friend, and you'd fit in good with all of us."

Pop arrived home around six. He came staggering in wearing his dirty uniform, streaked with grease. "What a day!" he gasped. "But we got all the beaters fixed and on their way. Darnell, that kid is a wonder. He's almost as good as me now. *Almost.*"

Chelsea, Athena, Keisha, and Lindall were all there to greet Pop. "Hey! Hey!" he cried. "There's Athena. Look at her. She's wearin' that top that falls over her shoulders all the time. Watch it there, Athena. You don't want to be standin' here with nothin' on the top, right?"

Chelsea giggled and nudged Lindall. Then she said, "Pop, this is my new friend, Lindall Giles."

"Hi there, Lindall," Pop replied. "Now here's a young lady dressed nice. Very beautiful. Nice little top there. The jeans, they don't look like you were squeezed into 'em like toothpaste. Nice. Good job, Lindall."

Pop turned to Keisha. "You're lookin' good too, Keisha. Only problem we got here is Athena, bustin' out of her too small clothes."

Lindall said in a serious voice, "My sister sometimes buys clothes that are too small, Mr. Spain."

Jaris, Chelsea, and Pop exchanged looks. They were bursting to laugh. Pop escaped to the bathroom to clean up.

The girls gathered in Chelsea's bedroom, and Lindall remarked, "Ohhh! I like your bedroom, Chelsea. It's so pretty, like mine used to be. My room was nice and big like this," Lindall noted. "I had a white chest of drawers and a big mirror. I felt like a princess. Now I have to share a room with my sister, and it's an ugly room. Denique hates it too."

"Thanks, Lindall. Mom let me pick out the paint colors myself." Then Chelsea thought about what Jaris had said about Denique. "Is Denique nice?" Chelsea asked.

"Sometimes," Lindall answered. "She was much nicer when we lived in the big house and had separate rooms. You know what, Chelsea? I like your brother. He seems really nice."

Chelsea was sure now that Denique had not mentioned the red-lacy-panty event to anybody in her family, certainly not to Lindall.

Marvelous aromas soon began to float from the kitchen as Pop worked. In honor of the sleepover and Chelsea's new friend, he was outdoing himself.

Pop spoke quietly to Mom in the kitchen. "That little girl, Lindall—Chelsea said she's been through some rough times. The father, the bum, he just took off and left them all sittin', and now they're livin' over on Grant. The mom's scroungin' for a livin', workin' in some downtown office.

Grant's not a good place for kids. Not a good place for anybody."

"I'm so proud of Chelsea for taking her under her wing," Mom commented. "Our kids are goodhearted, Lorenzo. You don't know how thrilled I am about that. Jaris always reaches out to new kids too. He brought Kevin Walker and Oliver Randall right into the group when they were strangers. I suppose as parents we've made our share of mistakes, Lorenzo. But we're raising kids with good hearts, and that is pretty wonderful."

Pop grinned at his wife and planted a kiss on her lips. He would have hugged her too, but his hands were full of pots and pans.

Soon, Pop was carrying the dishes to the table to the oohs and aahs of the guests. "We got here garlic parmesan potatoes," he explained. A large plate contained golden crispy wedges of potatoes in a spoke pattern around mashed potatoes with cream cheese. "And we got your roasted veggies here—carrots, zucchini and onions. And then we got the main deal here, your roast beef and rice."

Lindall's eyes seemed to double in size.

"You should be a chef, Mr. Spain," Athena told him. "You'd get rich."

"Hey," Pop quipped, "I keep telling Monie here, I'm gonna start servin' food at Spain's Auto Care. They won't mind waitin' a little longer for their beaters to get fixed up if good eats're comin' down the pike."

After the dinner, Chelsea and her friends stayed up late Friday night.

On Saturday at about noon, Pop made a stack of golden pancakes swimming in maple syrup. Then Jaris piled the girls into his Honda for the trips home. Jaris dropped off Athena first, then Keisha. Finally, he headed for Grant with Lindall.

"I had lotsa fun with Chelsea and her friends," Lindall told him. "I had the most fun since ... you know ... the bad stuff happened."

"I'm glad," Jaris replied. "You're a very nice house guest. You're welcome anytime."

"I wish you were *my* big brother," Lindall remarked.

Jaris smiled. "That's a nice thing to say, Lindall. That's a real compliment, and I appreciate it."

As they drew closer to Grant, Jaris felt sorry for Lindall. It was a graffiti-ridden hangout for gangbangers. Most of the people tried to keep things clean in the alleys behind the apartments. But enough losers tossed their garbage out to spoil it for everybody. The good people had to live with rotting sofa pillows, mattresses, and parts of junk cars. Rats lived in the debris. Jaris had seen them scurrying there.

"I don't like living where we live now," Lindall told him.

"Yeah, well, maybe you can move to a better place soon," Jaris suggested.

"Mom's trying to find a better job where she'll earn more money," Lindall said. "Then we could move."

Jaris pulled into the parking lot alongside the apartment where Lindall lived. It was Saturday, and idle guys were standing around, staring, smoking, drinking beer. They were waiting for the night, when the action started.

Jaris would have preferred not to go near Lindall's apartment. But he didn't want the girl to have to walk past those creeps. So, reluctantly, he walked with Lindall to her apartment door. He hoped her mom would answer, and he could quickly escape.

After entering the building, Jaris and Lindall walked up the steps to the second story. There was a small porch off the landing, and Mrs. Giles had set out two potted plants. They softened the starkness of the place. They were the only green living things on the whole side of the building.

"Hi," Mrs. Giles greeted, opening the door. She looked at her daughter. "You had a good time, honey?" she asked.

"Yes!" Lindall cried with enthusiasm, and Mrs. Giles stepped back. "You must be Jaris Spain. Come on in."

"Oh no!" Jaris thought. He hoped against hope that Denique was not home. He stepped into the small apartment. Everything was neat and clean. Mrs. Giles was doing her best to make it livable. Yellow flowers brightened up the kitchen table. The floor, though worn, was clean and shining.

"Denique," Mrs. Giles called out, "the Spain boy brought Lindall home."

Jaris froze. It was all he could do not to turn on his heel and race out the door. But he knew that was no option.

Denique emerged from the bedroom and came down the short hall. Her mother asked, "Have you met Jaris?"

"Yeah, he's in some of my classes at school," Denique muttered.

"Hi, Denique," Jaris said, feeling more uncomfortable by the minute. "Well, gotta be going. 'Bye, Lindall … Mrs. Giles!" He flew out the door and took the steps down two at a time. Denique's cold stare had made his blood turn frosty. He couldn't imagine why she was carrying her grudge so far. It wasn't as if he had done something that terrible. He just laughed at a bad time, and he tried to apologize. Most people would have laughed—at least Jaris thought so.

On his way home, Jaris stopped at Alonee Lennox's house. At school, he had seen Alonee talking to Denique several times. Maybe she could help Jaris understand what was going on with this girl.

Alonee was helping her little sister Lark with her homework. Then she saw Jaris in the driveway. She pulled a couple of ginger ales from the refrigerator and went outside to greet him. They sat down together on the front steps.

"What's happening, Jaris?" Alonee asked.

"Chelsea had a sleepover with her friends, and she invited Lindall Giles, Denique's little sister," Jaris answered.

"She's a sweet kid. But just now I dropped Lindall off at her place, and Denique looked at me like I was the devil. What's with her? Just 'cause me and Kevin laughed—"

"Well, you know Denique's father skipped out on the family, and she's bitter about that," Alonee told him. "She hates living over on Grant. She's just sorta mad at the world right now."

"But why is she so mad at *me*?" Jaris asked. "I mean, it wasn't nice that I laughed and stuff, but what's the big deal?"

"Jaris, you know," Alonee reasoned, "sometimes your whole world falls apart. You got nothing to hang onto except your anger. I think that's what's happening with Denique. She hates all her male teachers. She hates the boys at Tubman. She kinda sees her father in all the males in her life."

"Poor Lindall, living with that witchy sister," Jaris remarked. "Alonee, what can I do? I've already apologized to Denique, and she just threw it back at me."

Alonee smiled at Jaris and patted his shoulder. "You can't do anything, Jaris. You're such a good person that you're beating yourself over the head about what you did. But it's not about you. Even if you and Kevin hadn't laughed at Denique, she'd still be full of rage. We've just got to be nice to Denique until she can come outta the other side of this darkness she's in."

Jaris was quiet for a few moments, sipping on his ginger ale.

"Another thing, Alonee," Jaris commented. "I hardly see Trevor anymore. He was so lonely. Then he made a play for that Amberlynn at the Chicken Shack, and she blew him off. Now he doesn't even come to eat lunch with us anymore."

"Yeah, I know," Alonee agreed. "He hides behind the gym and eats his lunch sitting on one of those stone benches. I saw him one day, but I pretended I didn't. I didn't want to embarrass him."

"I'd try to fix him up with someone," Jaris said, "but Tommy tried that, and it was a disaster."

Jaris gulped the last of the soda and handed Alonee the can.

"Well, thanks for listening to me, Alonee," he told her. "You always make me feel better just by listening."

At lunchtime on Monday, Trevor again didn't go down under the eucalyptus trees with his friends. He found the same bench behind the gym. He had heated some soup in the school microwave, and he sat there slowly eating the chicken and noodles.

Overhead, crows were squawking at each other, and he watched them. He heard somewhere that crows were getting so plentiful that they were scaring off all the other birds. Trevor heard them cawing and then screeching in the trees. He wondered whether they were arguing. Maybe the male crows had trouble finding female crows. He felt sorry for them. No wonder they were in such a bad mood.

A shadow fell on the sidewalk in front of Trevor. He was sitting on the extreme right side of the bench, and a girl sat down far to the left. It was Denique Giles. Her lunch was two packages of peanut butter crackers.

"You waiting for anyone?" Denique Giles asked Trevor.

"Nope," he replied.

They ate their lunches for a minute or so.

"Alonee told me your father ditched you and your ma and your brothers," Denique remarked.

"Yeah," Trevor grunted.

"I bet you hated him, huh?" Denique suggested, fire in her eyes.

"Nah. I was just a baby. I never knew him," Trevor responded.

"Why'd he leave?" Denique asked, brushing cracker crumbs off the knees of her jeans.

"He got kicked out," Trevor told her. "Ma couldn't stand him usin' up all the money for booze. She hadda get rid of him."

"You ever see him?' the girl asked.

"I see him around town," Trevor said. "He's kinda homeless now. Begging for change, you know. He lives behind the stores. I never talk to him. When he sees me, he looks away, and I do too. He doesn't wanna talk to me, and I don't wanna talk to him. What's to say?"

"My father's an engineer," Denique volunteered. "He and Mom never argued much. I didn't think anything was wrong. My father went to work every day and earned good money. Mom worked part time, just for pin money, she'd say. Then he got weird. He wouldn't talk anymore. He'd come home from work and just sit there and not say anything. Then he left. He said he had to get away."

"That's rough, real rough," Trevor commented.

"Yeah, it just happened so fast," Denique went on. "Mom couldn't pay the mortgage on the house. We had a big mort- gage. The bank took our house then and all the furniture too. Mom got in touch with my father, but he wasn't working anymore. He was living with his old parents. He had no money. He wouldn't even talk to Mom. Grandma, Dad's mother, she said not to call anymore 'cause he had no money, and that was it. Mom tried going to court. But they got a lawyer for him, and he got off the hook. Grandma said you can't squeeze blood out of a turnip. That's what she said."

Trevor finished his soup and threw his trash into a plastic bag. He held the bag out for Denique to drop the cracker wrappers in. He looked at the girl. "Did you ever talk to your father since he left?" he asked.

"No. I hate him so much for what he did," Denique snarled. "He abandoned his family. He threw us to the wolves."

"He ever say good-bye to you kids or anything?" Trevor asked.

Denique shook her head. "He left a stupid little note. Later he texted us, me and Lindall. He kinda rambled. He said it was all over. He said he tried, but he couldn't help it. He said we should try to forgive him, but I never will. Maybe Lindall will 'cause she's a mushier person, but I never will. I'll always hate him for what he did."

Trevor shrugged. "Life's not fair," he observed. "I don't understand it. I don't understand people. If I could, I'd be up there on the poles with the crows. That's where I'd be."

CHAPTER SIX

Denique laughed a little. Trevor had never seen her laugh before. Laughter dramatically changed the appearance of her face. He was startled by how pretty she was when she laughed.

"You're the strangest guy I ever met, Trevor," Denique told him. "I mean, I never met a guy like you. You're like from another planet."

"Yeah?" Trevor responded. "I'm not surprised. I got some strange feelings. Like one time I read a book about crows. I found out they mostly go 'caw, caw,' but they got other sounds too. They like got a language like us, and the different sounds have different meanings."

They both stared at the crows and listened for a few seconds.

"Trevor, you're friends with Alonee Lennox, aren't you?" Denique asked.

"Yeah, I like her. She's kindhearted," Trevor replied.

"I like her too," Denique agreed. "But how come you got those rotten friends too, those guys, Jaris and Kevin. I've seen you hanging with those creeps. You're not like them, Trevor."

"Sure I am," Trevor objected. "Jaris is my best friend. He's like a brother to me. He's got my back no matter what trouble I'm in. Kevin's a good guy too."

"I used to see you going to lunch under the eucalyptus trees with those creeps, but now you don't anymore. How come?" Denique asked.

"I wanna be alone for a change," Trevor explained. "I just got tired of being with people."

That wasn't the true reason, of course. But he wasn't going to share his humiliating secret with a chick he hardly knew. He wasn't going to tell her about the emptiness and longing in his heart for a girl of his own. He couldn't admit how it broke his heart to see Jaris with Sereeta, Kevin with Carissa, Oliver with Alonee. He had nobody. Trevor was ashamed that he was a senior in high school and didn't have a girl.

He wasn't looking for a deep romantic relationship like the one between Jaris and Sereeta or even between Oliver and Alonee. He wanted something fun and casual, like Kevin and Carissa had. He wanted to like someone who liked him—to have fun.

Trevor wanted to lie on the grass under the eucalyptus trees and put his head in a girl's lap, as Kevin did with Carissa. He wanted to come on campus in the morning and see his chick and maybe walk hand in hand with her.

Trevor wanted to take his girl to the beach and romp in the waves with her, as Jaris and Sereeta did. Trevor had taken Vanessa Allen to the beach, and they watched the sun go down together. But she didn't even like him. He wanted a girl who truly liked him.

But Trevor was too embarrassed to share any of that with Denique. Then, out of the blue, Denique asked, "You got a girlfriend? I know you said you hated chicks, but I thought maybe you had one you liked."

"Nobody. I'm too busy for that stuff anyway," he answered gruffly. "I work at the Chicken Shack, and I have to spend a lot of time studyin' to get good grades. I wanna be able to go to college and support myself. Ma isn't gonna be able to help much. I don't even have a car. I borrow my brother's Cavalier when I need to go somewhere. I wanna get my own wheels—"

"I sorta had a boyfriend where I lived before," Denique interrupted. "But he turned out to be a jerk. That soured me on dating."

"I sorta had a girlfriend too," Trevor admitted. "I bet she was a bigger jerk than your boyfriend."

Denique laughed again. Trevor enjoyed seeing her laugh. "We are weirdly alike, Trevor," she noted. "Maybe we both came from the same faraway galaxy." Then she got serious. "I need a part-time job so I can help Mom. You know any place who'd hire a dummy like me who can't do anything?"

"The Ice House," Trevor answered quickly. "That's a yogurt place. They don't pay much, but kids always comin' and goin'. Go and fill out an application. Maybe they'll hire you."

When Denique called herself a dummy, Trevor might have said something like, "You're not a dummy." But he didn't. And he didn't even realize he might have insulted her.

But he didn't. Denique took no offense. "Easier said than done," she responded. "I catch the bus from Tubman over to that lousy neighborhood where I live. Mom has no car. How would I get to this Ice House to even ask for a job?"

"I got my brother's car today," Trevor told her. "He let me borrow it 'cause I gotta work tonight. You wanna go to the Ice House and make out an application?"

"Yeah, you mean you could drive me over there?" Denique asked.

"Sure. Meet me in the parking lot after classes," Trevor replied. "I'll take you over there. Like I said, crummy pay, but the kids our age don't usually make much."

After school, Denique was waiting at the Cavalier as Trevor walked up to it. Trevor did a double-take. The girl looked good. She had dark curly hair that framed a cute face. When she wasn't scowling, which she usually was, she looked cute. Her lips were full and pouty. But the minute those thoughts came into his mind, Trevor dismissed them. He wasn't going down that road again. All Denique wanted from him was a ride to the Ice House to look for a job. Period. She hated guys. She thought they were jerks. Trevor was just another jerk.

Trevor didn't bother to hold the door open for Denique as he did for Amberlynn Parson at the Chicken Shack. He had been trying to impress Amberlynn, but it didn't work. Chicks didn't care whether a guy was polite. They wanted somebody hot like Jaris or Oliver or Kevin. Trevor wasn't hot, and he never would be. Chicks wanted guys like Jaris with smoky eyes and charisma. They wanted bad boys like Kevin with his hot temper that sent off sparks or smooth guys like Oliver. They didn't want dorks. So Trevor let Denique let herself into the Cavalier before he drove off.

Trevor and Denique went into the Ice House together. They ordered frozen strawberry yogurts and ate them at a table while she filled out the application.

"They wanna know about work experience," Denique groaned. "Like I've got any. I never had to work before. My father made good money. I babysat a few times, but that's not gonna help on this stupid application. I'm seventeen years old, and I've never worked!"

"Well," Trevor suggested, "put that down. The babysitting. At least it's somethin'."

While he spoke, Trevor's gaze drifted toward the girls behind the counter. This store is where he met Vanessa Allen. She really came on to him. He was in heaven. She was so sweet, so pretty. He couldn't believe his good fortune when she seemed to actually like him. Now the memory brought him only sadness.

"I'll turn this in, but it's a waste," Denique grumbled. "Why would they want me when I got no experience?"

As they walked out, Trevor offered to drop Denique home on his way to work.

"That'd be nice," Denique said. "I hate taking that stupid bus. By the time I get on, most of the seats are taken. If I do find a seat, some creep squeezes in next to me. I hate riding the bus. We had two cars in our family where I used to live. My mother

102

would drop me at school and pick me up. She and my father promised me they'd buy me a car when I turned seventeen. Ha!"

"It's harder to put up with stuff when you've had it better," Trevor commented. "We've always been up against it in my family. For me, it kinda seems normal."

As they neared Grant, Trevor noticed the girl looking at him, making him uncomfortable. What was she thinking? Was it, "Poor fool. He said he was too busy to have a girlfriend, but who would *want* him? A nerd like him?" That was probably what she was thinking. A lot of girls were mean like that. Girls were like Marko Lane. He stood around Tubman, rating the girls, giving them scores of one to ten. The girls he called "dogs" were ones. Girls did the same thing, only in their minds.

It would be dusk in a few hours. Guys were already hanging around on the street corners. Soon they'd be out tagging and looking for trouble. They'd be looking to jump some poor fool who stumbled onto the wrong street wearing the wrong colors.

"Thanks for the ride home," Denique said when Trevor stopped the car in front of her apartment. She didn't get out right away. She seemed to want to say something else but was having a hard time saying it. Finally, she turned to him.

"Trevor," she began nervously, "you said you were too busy for a girlfriend and you don't like girls anyway. But of all the boys I've met at Tubman High, you're the only one I'd say this to. Oh!"

She sighed in frustration.

"What am I trying to say?" she went on. "I really don't want a boyfriend, and you don't want a girlfriend, and that's cool. But if you ever want somebody to just hang with on the weekend, and you don't know anybody else to ask, you could call me. I'd probably say yes. So, anyway,"—she was writing on a scrap of paper—"here's the phone number. I've never done this before in my life, but you're pretty cool, Trevor."

Trevor took the slip of paper with her number on it. His mind was spinning, and he was speechless. Denique didn't say another thing. She just got out of the car and vanished into the apartment building.

"*What did she say?*" he asked himself.

Trevor kept trying to convince himself that she really didn't say what he heard her say. But there was her scrawled phone number. Still, there had to be some mistake. She was too pretty to suggest that she might actually go out with Trevor.

Trevor sat there for a few minutes. He folded the slip of paper and put it carefully into his shirt pocket. Finally, he drove toward the Chicken Shack, still in a fog.

That same evening, Chelsea was downloading music in her room when Athena called. "I'm having a party at my house Saturday, Chel. You absolutely gotta come 'cause you're my best friend," Athena told her breathlessly. "Keisha and Lindall and Inessa are coming, and Heston

Crawford and Maurice Moore. Most of the kids can come on bikes or walk. But I asked Vic to pick up Lindall 'cause he drives a motorcycle. It's gonna be in the afternoon, Chelsea, and it's gonna be awesome."

Chelsea felt excited about the party, and she wanted to go. But she was nervous too. Pop had already told her many times that Athena's house was off-limits for parties or sleepovers. Bad things happened over there, Pop declared with a dark look on his face. But surely he might relent about an afternoon party where *all* of Chelsea's friends were going. "I gotta ask my parents, Athena. Mom isn't home, but Pop is," Chelsea told her friend.

"Chel, don't tell your father about Vic coming," Athena pleaded. "You know how ballistic he got when he caught me kissing Vic that morning. But Vic's a really nice guy. Just tell your father it's gonna be girls and a couple freshman boys."

"I'll call you right back, Athena," Chelsea promised.

Pop was watching the news on TV. "Bunch of liars are all they are," he was yelling at the screen. He turned to look at Chelsea as she entered the living room. He pointed at the screen. "Advertise all this stuff," he started to rant. "Supposed to make you beautiful, healthy, like a kid again. But they tell you about the side effects real fast so maybe you'll miss it. Like they go, 'All your wrinkles disappear.' Then real quick they say the stuff might make your face blow up like a balloon. And if that happens, get to your doctor fast."

"Pop," Chelsea said fast, when her father paused to take a breath. "Athena's having a party on Saturday. Everybody's going."

"What makes that news send chills up my spine, little girl?" Pop asked, using the remote to kill the TV.

"It's gonna be Keisha and Inessa and just girls we hang with, Pop," Chelsea assured him.

"Chelsea, you ain't goin' to no party at Athena's house," Pop declared. "I thought we got all that settled a long time ago. I don't like the way those idiot parents run that house. I been over there to find Athena all by her lonesome except for some punk kissing her up. That's right, some older punk who's got no business with a fourteen-year-old. I been there when she's all alone and swings the door wide open when the doorbell rings. That doorbell ringer could be some maniac for all she knows. No way. If everybody is gettin' together, let them come over here. I'll even cook brownies for them."

"Pop, it's going to be a great party, and—" Chelsea started to whine.

"Oh, I bet it'll be that all right," Pop responded, with a wag of his head. "Now you mentioned a coupla girls, nice girls like Keisha and Inessa, but let me guess. Some little boy punks are gonna be crawling through the cracks in the door. Maybe even that bum I found with Athena's orangey lipstick all over his pimply face that morning. Yeah, I bet he's comin' to the party for sure. Forget it, little girl. Tell Athena the party's gonna be here or at Keisha's house or Inessa's, or you ain't goin'. Period. End of story."

Mom had come home, and, even from the driveway, she'd heard the loud voice in the living room.

"Mom!" Chelsea wailed. "Athena is having a nice party for all of us at her house Saturday afternoon, and Pop won't let me go! Mommm, everybody's gonna be there!"

Mom glanced over at Pop. "Honey," she said to Chelsea, "I want for you to have fun, but couldn't the girls come over here? We wouldn't mind the whole gang coming over—"

"Mom, Athena wants the party at her house, and she's got all her plans made," Chelsea cried.

"I bet she does have wonderful plans," Pop yelled. "Maybe a buncha punks comin' from college with kegs of beer. It ain't gonna happen, little girl. Athena's a loose cannon, and her parents are idiots. I'm not letting you go to no party at the Edson house."

Chelsea turned and stomped off to her room. She sat in her chair with her arms folded until she'd calmed down a little. Then she called Athena.

"My pop won't let me come, Athena. *I begged him*," Chelsea groaned.

"Oh, Chelsea, it's not gonna be near as much fun if you're not here," Athena told her.

"I know, and I want to come so bad," Chelsea agreed.

"Chelsea, listen," Athena said, "it's not fair that they won't let you come. Why don't you tell your parents that you're biking down to the library on Saturday? The party's around three o'clock. Just come over here instead."

Chelsea thought for a moment. She often biked down to the library on Saturday afternoons. It would be easy to head that way and then just turn the corner to Athena's house. Mom and Pop would never

know the difference. Then another thought
struck Chelsea.

"Athena," she told her friend, "I just
got over being grounded for riding in that
car with those dopesters when we were
finishing middle school. I don't want to
get into trouble again." Last year, Chelsea
and Athena and Keisha were lured into a
hundred-mile-an-hour trip around town
in a car driven by drug dealers who sam-
pled their own product. Pop was so furi-
ous he took away all Chelsea's rights. She
couldn't walk to and from school, and she
couldn't ride her bike. She was so happy
when she started Tubman, and she got
back her rights. Now she turned it over in
her mind whether that party at Athena's
was worth the risk.

"Oh, Athena," Chelsea groaned. She
was torn between going to Athena's party
and not risking Pop's wrath.

"Chelsea, Heston Crawford is coming,"
Athena said. "I told him you'd be here, and
he said he'd come just to be with you. He's

counting on you being there. He said he might not even come if you're not coming."

Chelsea really liked Heston. Recently, when they were walking in the early evening, he planted a quick kiss on Chelsea's lips. She felt all goose bumpy all night. The thought of Heston being at the party made it all the harder to resist. And *everybody* was going to be there. It didn't seem fair that everybody but Chelsea Spain could go to this great party.

"Lemme think, Athena," Chelsea said. "Lemme just think. I'll call you back."

Chelsea made her decision. She was going to pretend to go to the library on Saturday afternoon. First she'd stop whining about not being allowed to go to the party. Then she'd start talking about a big project she had and how she needed to spend some time at the library. She'd say she had to use books that the library did not lend out. You had to read them in the library. Pop would ask Chelsea why she couldn't research her project on the Internet. Then she'd explain that some important stuff was in those books at the library. Chelsea could say the librarian had put the books aside for her to look at.

Chelsea felt bad plotting to fool her parents. Her parents, especially Pop, were so dead set against her being at Athena's house. And yet what could be wrong with going to a party on Saturday afternoon with *all* her friends? It was ridiculous! Keisha, Inessa, Lindall, Falisha, and everybody else would be there, but Chelsea could not. Didn't their parents care about them? Keisha's parents were very strict, yet she could go. Inessa's parents were really strict, and she'd be there.

Chelsea called Athena back. "Your parents are gonna be there, right?" she asked.

"Well," Athena answered, "not my dad. He has to see a client, but Mom'll be there. She's getting her hair and nails done Saturday morning, but she'll be there for the party. Chelsea, it's not that we're doing something bad. We're gonna play music

113

and maybe watch a movie on the big-screen TV. We're gonna have some super snacks. It'll be over around six, and everybody can go home before it's dark. The library stays open until seven on Saturday, so that'll cover you."

"Okay," Chelsea agreed, her heart pounding. "I think I'm gonna come, Athena. I might not stay the whole time, but I'll be there."

"Great!" Athena exclaimed. "Oh, Chel, you won't be sorry. We're gonna have three awesome party platters that Mom's getting for us. We got ham and cheese and little tarts and sparkling apple cider. I just want you to be part of the fun, girl, 'cause you're my bestie."

"Yeah, I know," Chelsea responded. "I'll be there!"

"All right!" Athena cried.

Chelsea was thinking about the party the whole rest of the week. At school, she learned that Inessa was having second thoughts about going. "My parents don't want me to go," Inessa confided. "I don't know if I'm goin' or not."

Keisha told pretty much the same thing to Chelsea. "I had to promise my parents that if anything went wrong I'd call them right away to come get me. I'm really nervous about going."

Inessa gave Chelsea a cold, hard look. "How come your pop is letting you go to Athena's party, Chelsea? He's the strictest of all our fathers. I can't believe he's gonna let you go."

Chelsea was ashamed to admit that she was planning to fool her father with a phony story about going to the library on Saturday. "Pop says I'm almost fifteen, and he's decided to trust me," Chelsea lied. "He said he knows I'll leave the party right away if anything isn't right. Pop says I'm trustworthy now. I know how to behave myself."

"That don't sound like your pop," Inessa sniffed. "He's scary. I can't imagine him sayin' stuff like that. You sure you heard him right, Chelsea?"

"Yes," Chelsea insisted. "He's sorta changing ... he, uh ... knows I'm more responsible now and stuff like that." Chelsea felt her face growing warm.

On Friday night, Chelsea had trouble sleeping. What she was planning to do on Saturday upset her very much. She loved and respected Pop. She hated fooling him, especially on something he felt so strongly about. She had nightmares of him looking at her with hurt and rage in his eyes. She tossed and turned, woke up at two a.m., and couldn't get back to sleep. She kept hearing Pop's aggrieved voice, "Little girl, how could you?" But it wasn't Pop's voice. It was the wind outside the half open window.

Chelsea looked across the room. She had assembled all her notes on her project.

The project was about the young poets who died in World War I. More young poets died during World War I than in any war in history. Chelsea was writing about them for her project, particularly about Joyce Kilmer and Wilfred Owen. She had told her parents that she would be studying a special book on Wilfred Owen. Chelsea said that this Saturday afternoon study period was really important in making a good grade in world history. That's why she had to leave around two thirty, and they needn't expect her home until around six.

Since Chelsea *was* writing a project on the poets, she wasn't telling a complete lie. That made her feel a little better. The truth, however, was that she was already done with most of her research. She had read several books and gotten a lot off the Internet. In fact, she had already gathered and printed it.

CHAPTER SEVEN

At breakfast, Chelsea had no appetite. Mom smiled at her and said, "You have to eat a good breakfast, sweetheart. You have a big day ahead at the library. Your brain works better if you're well nourished."

"Yeah," Pop added. "That project you're doing on those poets sounds like a good one, little girl. I read about those guys when I went to school. One of those poets—I think he was from Canada—name o' McCrae, I think. He wrote this poem, 'In Flanders Fields.' He was like saying when the soldier dies and gets buried, they plant these poppies between the crosses in the cemetery. Real touchin' poem."

Pop took a long drink of coffee, then he looked right at Chelsea, "Y'know, Chelsea, lot better thing goin' to the library and finishin' your project. Lot better than goin' to that airhead Athena's party. You'll be busy workin' there at the library and won't be feelin' bad about missin' all those shenanigans. I got a bad feelin' about that party anyway, little girl."

Chelsea finally finished her bran flakes, eggs, and orange juice. She looked at the clock on the kitchen wall. Nine. She wouldn't be leaving for the party for hours. She had all that time to worry and feel guilty.

Chelsea wanted to wear something cute to the party, but she thought that would make Pop suspicious. If she wore one of her pretty new tops, he'd wonder what was going on. Who dressed up to go to the library?

Chelsea tried different tops on. When it was close to the time she was leaving, she slipped on a really striking tank top. Then she pulled a long-sleeved sweatshirt over it. At the party, she just needed to pull off the sweatshirt.

Chelsea put her school binder in her tote bag. She was growing more nervous by the minute. She had always promised her parents she'd be truthful with them. Now she was totally going against her promise. She felt awful. And yet she didn't want to miss Athena's party, especially since Heston was coming just for Chelsea.

"Well, I guess I'm going," Chelsea announced.

"Good luck on your research, sweetie," Mom told her. It made Chelsea feel even worse that her parents believed her.

"Yeah, little girl, do a bang up job," Pop added.

Only Jaris looked at Chelsea in a strange way. Chelsea figured maybe he suspected something; that he thought something was wrong. But he didn't say anything. Chelsea smiled at Jaris and spoke to him pointedly. "When I get all my research together, Jaris, maybe you can read it and help me put on the finishing touches."

"Sure, chili pepper, be glad to," Jaris agreed.

"Well, good-bye, you guys," Chelsea called out.

Chelsea's legs felt watery as she went out to get her bike. She climbed astride it and pedaled. She kept telling herself that her parents were being ridiculous and unfair by not letting let her go to Athena's party. If they had been reasonable, she wouldn't have been driven to do something underhanded like this. Actually, Chelsea told herself, this was her parents' fault, not hers.

Chelsea biked down the street, heading for the intersection of Iroquois Street. A right turn would take her quickly to Athena's house. Going left would lead to the library, where everybody thought she was going.

Chelsea thought about Heston Crawford and how glad he'd be to see her. She smiled when she thought of Heston. If she didn't go to the party, poor Heston would be looking for her and feeling really disappointed. Even if she had no other reason for going to the party, having a good time with Heston would be reason enough.

Chelsea reached the intersection and stood with her bike, waiting for the light to change. Many emotions swirled in her heart. Her parents trusted that she was going to the library, even though it was exactly same time as Athena's party. That's how much they trusted her.

Chelsea remembered something that Athena had said to her once. "Your father's like a bear, like a big old wild bear fighting for his cub. I mean, like the whole world is a dark, dangerous place, and he's gotta watch out for you all the time, that's how he acts."

Right after saying that, Athena had gotten a forlorn look on her face. Then she said, "He loves you a lot." At that moment, Chelsea got the feeling that Athena believed Chelsea's father loved her more than

Athena's father loved his daughter. And, for all her risk taking and bravado, Athena seemed to envy Chelsea her father's love.

The light changed. Chelsea didn't move, seeing her father's angry, sorrowful face when he found out she had betrayed him. And maybe he *would* find out. He might never trust Chelsea again. But even if Pop never found out, Chelsea would know what she did, and the memory would hurt.

Chelsea started to shake. She got up on the bike and pedaled it to a start. The intersection was only a few feet away. In a second, she would have to turn.

She turned left, toward the library.

She couldn't believe she was doing it, but she was. She pedaled fast toward the library. She got off her bike and wheeled it into the bike rack, locking it. Then she got on her cell phone.

"Heston," she told him, "I just wanted you to know I'm not going to Athena's party. I was gonna go, but my parents are really dead set against it. So I'm not goin', and I didn't want you to be looking for me, Heston."

"Awww! Okay, girl. Thanks for letting me know," Heston responded. "I didn't wanna go either, Chelsea, but I thought I'd go if you were there. See you at school, Chelsea."

Then Chelsea called Athena. "Athena, I'm sorry, but I can't make it. I can't trick my parents, especially Pop. He'd be so hurt if he found out. I just couldn't face him. I'm sorry, Athena."

"Boy, what a friend you are!" Athena snapped bitterly. "My best friend in the whole world, and you're missing the best party I ever had. You're such a chicken, Chelsea. You're a silly daddy's little girl, and you make me sick!"

Tears filled Chelsea's eyes. "Athena, I want so much to come to your party, but I just can't—" she cried.

"You said they bought the story about you going to the library, Chelsea," Athena insisted. "Nobody would ever be the wiser.

They'd never find out. Come on, girl, you can do it. Your parents are so unfair. They're ruining your whole life. Y'hear what I'm saying, girl?"

"Yeah, Athena, and maybe you're right, but I just can't." Chelsea was sticking to her guns.

"Okay, then," Athena responded in a prissy voice. "Be a good little girl, and miss the best party in this whole freakin' neighborhood. Everybody else is gonna be here, and they'll tell you at school all what you missed. You know what, Chelsea? Your parents should put an ankle bracelet on you, like with people on parole. They could track you with a GPS. You might as well be in jail!"

Chelsea had never heard Athena so angry. Tears ran down her face. She didn't want to hurt Athena. She really was Chelsea's best friend. Chelsea almost changed her mind again, jumped on her bike, and took off for Athena's party. But she didn't. She grabbed her tote bag and walked into the library, her shoulders slumping and her head down. She was sad and angry.

Chelsea didn't know that Jaris had parked several blocks from the library. He'd walked to a brushy area across from the library and waited. He'd been watching for about ten minutes when he saw Chelsea pull up on her bike, park it, and lock it. Of course, she was on the phone, but why not? She wouldn't be able to use the phone in the library. She'd probably go into phone deprivation shock.

Jaris smiled then and walked back to his Honda. He had had a strong suspicion that Chelsea was lying about her trip to the library. She had guilt all over her face at the breakfast table. Jaris was almost sure that she would head for Athena's house and that the library trip was just a cover story. Well, he figured he was wrong. Now, Jaris had new respect for his little sister. She kept her word and was actually going into the library.

"Way to go, chili pepper," Jaris whispered under his breath.

He would never tell her he had been spying on her today. Never.

Jaris went home and did some work on his AP American History class. Pop made a late lunch of chili dogs for everyone. They were just finishing eating when the phone rang. It was about three thirty.

"Hi," Jaris said, but the pleasant look on his face soon evaporated. "*What?* Lindall, stop crying. I can't even understand what you're saying. Tell me what's happening?"

Mom looked up, a frown on her face. "What's the matter?" she asked. "What's going on?"

Jaris didn't answer his mother. He held up his hand to have Mom wait a moment. He was focused on calming Lindall down. "Listen, honey, stop crying," he was saying in a soothing voice. "It's okay. We'll be over there in a coupla minutes, and we'll take you home. I promise. Yeah, we're just a few blocks over from there. You're outside, sitting on the steps? That's good,

Lindall. Stay there. Stay put. I'll be there in a few minutes. I'm leaving right now."

"What's wrong?" Pop growled.

"Lindall is at the party at Athena's house," Jaris reported. "She's really scared. She wants to go home. I don't know what's going on, Pop, but it's not good."

Pop snatched his truck keys off the wall. "You go in your car, and I'll follow in the truck, boy. I knew that little twit Athena was up to no good. That's why I wouldn't let our little girl go over there. I'll bet you Trudy Edson ain't nowhere around either. I'm tellin' you, that kid and her crazy parents are a menace to society." Pop was storming.

As Jaris turned the corner to Athena's house, he spotted Lindall sitting on the front steps. Loud music was blasting from the house. The entire house seemed to be pulsing to the music. It sounded like a hundred amps all going at once. Jaris pulled into the driveway, and Pop came in right behind him.

Lindall was sobbing. Jaris knelt in front of her and spoke to her softly. "It's okay now. We're going home, little girl." He surprised himself for a moment; he was starting to sound just like Pop.

"I t-tried to c-call M-mom," Lindall wept. She was speaking between sobs. "But she … she didn't answer. I guess she had to go to work. Jaris, the k-kids in there are wild. I got so s-scared. They're acting funny, s-some of them."

Jaris took Lindall to his car and buckled her into the passenger seat. Then he turned to Pop. "I'm taking her home. She's really freaked out. If her mother or sister isn't home, I'll stay with her until somebody shows up. What're you gonna do, Pop?"

Pop's eyes were smoldering. He glanced at the Edson house. "I'm takin' the fun house down, boy," Pop fumed. "I'm goin' in that madhouse and runnin' the inmates out. I'm callin' Trudy Edson if she ain't there—and what do ya wanna bet she ain't? I'm tellin' her I'm callin' the cops on her if what's goin' on in there is what I think is goin' on. I'm gonna put the fear o' the Lord in that idiot woman's heart."

Lorenzo Spain hit the doorbell to the Edson house. Nobody came. He rapped. The door swung open. It hadn't been locked. He saw about six girls and five boys. Some of them were dancing. A few were sprawled on the couches, drinking something. Pop looked around for any sign of Trudy Edson. He didn't see her, so he walked up to Athena, who was dancing in the arms of Vic Stevens. Vic looked drunk.

"Hey, punk," Pop shouted at the boy, "get lost!" Pop jerked a thumb in the air to emphasize the point.

Vic let go of Athena and backed off to the other side of the room.

"Athena," Pop demanded, "where's your mother?"

"She … uh … had to go in to the school, Mr. Spain," Athena answered. She looked a little bleary-eyed. She smiled and suggested,

"Have some refreshments. Everything's so yummy."

"Hey, Athena," Pop declared, "wonderful party you got goin' here. Beautiful."

Pop looked around the room, hands on hips and bobbing his head up and down. He recognized Maurice Moore and Keisha sitting over in the corner, but no other friends of Chelsea's seemed to be there. Chelsea had said "everybody" was coming, but there was no sign of Inessa, Falisha, or Heston.

Pop shouted an order to a boy with an orange streak in his hair. "Turn down the freakin' music, dude, or I'll kick your woofers to kingdom come."

Silence was quickly restored to the house. Kids who had been laughing and partying moments before now looked serious. They couldn't have looked more grim than if the cops were at the door.

"Keisha, what're you doin' here?" Pop demanded. "How come your parents let you come here?"

"I didn't know it'd be like this, Mr. Spain," Keisha murmured, hanging her head. "Some guys brought beer and vodka."

"You lied to your folks, right?" Pop growled. "You told 'em you were goin' somewhere else and you ended up here."

Pop glanced around the room, turning on his heel. He didn't recognize most of the kids. They were from Tubman, but they were juniors. Most of them, including Athena, were a little buzzed.

Pop turned to Athena, "Your mom got her cell with her?"

Athena nodded, and Pop called her.

"Hi there!" Trudy Edson answered in a cheerful teacher voice.

"Hey, Trudy, this is Lorenzo Spain, and I'm in your house here," Pop announced. "The kids're havin' a ball, Trudy. Beer, vodka, you name it. Athena, she's half shot, lookin' at me like an idiot. What're you doin', lady—lettin' somethin' like this happen? They got Margarita mix, and they're whipping up more drinks."

"What? What are you talking about, Mr. Spain?" Mrs. Edson gasped. "Athena said she was having a few of her little friends over. I bought party platters and soda pop."

"You still needed at the school, lady?" Pop asked. "You spendin' the day there?"

"Mr. Spain, I resent your speaking to me in that tone of voice," Mrs. Edson replied in a cold and cross voice. "I've done nothing wrong. I'm at the mall doing a little shopping. I saw nothing wrong in letting Athena and her friends … I thought they'd be having lemonade and cookies."

"They ain't messin' with no lemonade and cookies, Trudy," Pop snarled. "Lissen up, lady. You get your butt back here in fifteen minutes, or I'm callin' the cops. Your daughter is pie-eyed, and the rest of 'em ain't so good either. You got no business letting a loose cannon like Athena alone to run a party. Especially with junior punks from Tubman haulin' in the booze. You hear me? You get over here. Or I'm tellin' the cops this here unfit mom has turned her house over to a bunch of drunken kids."

"I'm leaving the mall immediately," Mrs. Edson stated in a frightened voice.

"See that you are," Pop insisted. "Or you'll be explaining all this to some nice people wearin' badges."

Pop put down the phone and turned to Athena. "Your mother—if we can call her that—is coming home quick. The rest of you, get on your cells and call your parents to come get you. You'll wanna do that 'cause when the cops get here, you don't wanna be still swimmin' in the Margarita bowl."

"I got my motorcycle parked outside," Vic Stevens offered nervously.

"Don't even think about drivin', punk," Pop stormed. "I seen your bike sittin' out there, and it ain't movin' with you. Call your parents, all of you. Except Keisha. I'll take you home."

Less than a half hour later, Trudy Edson was running up the walk, as a mother was escorting her unsteady sixteen-year-old son down the driveway. Other parents were arriving quickly. Pop heard bitter words between parents and kids as mothers and fathers collected their boys and girls. One mother, leading her fourteen-year-old daughter, glared at Mrs. Edson.

"Trudy! How did this happen?" the mother demanded. "When I told Maribeth she could come to this party, I assumed there'd be adult supervision!"

"I was here," Mrs. Edson lied. "I just stepped out for a few minutes." Mrs. Edson rushed into the house and confronted Athena. "I am so disappointed in you, Athena," she groaned.

"Yeah," Pop chimed in, his eyes comically bugged out. "Who knew? It's not like the kid ever done something like this before. Now all of a sudden she's runnin' wild. Who'da thunk it?"

"Athena, what happened?" Mrs. Edson asked. "You promised me you would be responsible here."

"I'm sick, Mom. I think I have to puke," Athena announced, fleeing toward the bathroom.

"All the booze comin' up," Pop observed. "That's good, she's gettin' it outta her system."

Sickening sounds erupted from the bathroom.

"Oooh, lissen!" Pop urged, holding a cupped hand to his ear. "She's in there heavin'. You wanna go in there and pretend you're a mother? Y'know, help the kid."

"Mr. Spain, you have no right to come into my house and speak to me in that abusive fashion," Trudy Edson asserted. "I happen to be a professional woman, and I am accustomed to being treated with respect!"

"Well, a thousand pardons there, Trudy," Pop apologized falsely. "But you see, one of them poor little girls, Lindall Giles, she ain't used to this high life. She got scared and called my house. So me and my son come over here to get her. Now

I'm takin' Keisha home, but I got a coupla more things to say to you, *professional
lady*. These are fourteen-, fifteen-year-old
kids here, except for the sixteen-year-old
punks. You got it?"

Pop dropped his head and turned his
body around completely in frustration. His
arms flapped once on his hips. He wagged
his head.

"They're stupid!" he almost shouted.
"They need supervision. You can't leave
them on their own. Y'hear what I'm sayin'?
That's what parents are for, y'know? That's
our job, Trudy. You're ... how old? Forty
maybe, or gettin' there fast. You get no
sense in all that time, lady? You're supposed to be an adult. You're a mother,
Trudy. What's *wrong* with you?"

Pop looked at Keisha, who was hiding
in a far corner. "Come on, Keisha, let's go. I
got a few things to say to your parents too."

As Pop and Keisha walked to the pickup
truck, Keisha made a confession. "I sorta
lied, Mr. Spain. I told my parents me and

Athena and Falisha were gonna be studying for a test in science."

"Oh yeah, that figures," Pop replied. "I know your father wouldna let you go to no party thrown by Athena."

Lorenzo Spain spotted Maurice Moore getting on his bicycle. "Hey, Maurice, you help yourself to any of that vodka in there?" he called out.

The boy turned. He looked sober. "Nah, Mr. Spain, I hate the taste of booze."

"That's good, very good," Pop said. Lorenzo Spain looked around. Vic Stevens's mother was driving Vic home, and his father was picking up his son's motorcycle. Pop smiled in satisfaction.

Keisha belted herself in alongside Lorenzo Spain, and they drove off. Tears started running down Keisha's face. She made a full confession.

"I asked my parents if I could go to a party at Athena's house, and they said no," she admitted tearfully. "Then I told them that the party was canceled, and me and

Athena and Falisha were gonna study together for a test instead. I didn't want to lie to them, but Athena told me everybody else was coming, even Chelsea. I was expecting to see Chelsea, Mr. Spain. I thought if you were letting Chelsea go, then it must be okay."

"When I let Chelsea go to *anything* at the Edson house, that'll be the day little pigs put on tuxedos and go dancing with beavers in top hats," Pop declared.

Keisha was upset about how the party turned out. And she was really nervous about what her parents would do when they got to her house. But still, a giggle almost broke out when she pictured pigs and beavers dancing together.

When Pop took Keisha into her parents' house, both her mother and father were there. Keisha tearfully told them about her lie and about what was going on at Athena's party.

"Child," Keisha's mother responded sadly, "it just hurts me so much that you lied to us. Go to your room now, and don't you come out until I call you."

"Yeah, Mom," Keisha whimpered, wiping her eyes.

Keisha's father stood there, shaking his head.

"Lorenzo," he said to Pop, "we do our best. When our daughters, yours and mine, went riding with that boy in the Mercedes, we grounded Keisha just like you did with Chelsea. But Keisha promised she would be honest with us, and she wouldn't do nothin' stupid again. What do we do, Lorenzo? You gotta ease up on the rules and trust them eventually."

"I hear ya, Abner," Pop agreed.

"Chelsea, she didn't go to the party, did she?" Keisha's father asked.

"No, she wanted to, though," Lorenzo Spain replied. "She begged us to let her go. She seemed really upset when Monie and I stood our ground. Then a little bit later, she comes and tells us she's goin' to the library to study for a project this afternoon, same time the party is goin' on."

Pop rolled his eyes.

"Sounded a little fishy that all of a sudden she decides to go to the library when the party is goin' on," he went on. "Monie and me, we had our doubts. We thought maybe our little girl was foolin' us, just like Keisha fooled you. So we asked our boy, Jaris, to check on her. He was to stay outta sight but to make sure she showed up at the library, like she said. Jaris done that, and he called us when he saw her goin' into the library."

Pop cocked his head and spoke warmly with his fellow parent. "Y'hear what I'm sayin', Abner. Trust 'em, but not too much."

"You spied on her?" Abner asked with a pained look on his face.

"Yeah, we did, and I ain't apologizing to anybody for it, Ab," Lorenzo Spain admitted. "Hey, they're kids. They don't always make the right calls. Sometimes they decide to do something risky, and it could cost 'em. What if Chelsea or Keisha went ridin' with one of those drunken punks at the party. I'm not lettin' that happen, even if I got to spy once in a while."

CHAPTER EIGHT

When Jaris was driving Lindall to Grant, she got to talking. "When Athena invited me to her party, I was so excited. Athena said Chelsea was gonna be there and all our friends. Chelsea is my very best friend, Jaris. I wanted to be there if she was gonna be there. So I asked my mom, and she said okay. Some boy, he picked me up. I thought it'd be a nice party, but then everybody started drinking and talking funny and I got scared. I didn't know anybody except Keisha and Maurice, and they weren't too happy either."

"Lindall, listen," Jaris advised. "Athena's a nice girl. She's got a good heart, but her parents are kinda goofy. They let her do whatever

143

she wants. Like Athena'll hang out nights at the twenty-four-seven store. That's dangerous. Athena takes a lotta risks. You gotta be careful with Athena, Lindall. You don't know the ropes yet, but from now on, don't go to Athena's house. She's a lot of fun when she comes to our house or some other girl's house, but you don't wanna be hangin' at her place. Her parents are never there, and Athena kinda runs wild."

"I tried to call Mom to come get me," Lindall murmured, still weepy. "But she sometimes works Saturdays at different jobs. She's a temp. She makes extra money if she works on Saturday. I couldn't reach Denique. And we got no regular phone in the house. Just the mobile phones. Then I remembered you guys, and I figured you'd help me."

"Anytime you got a problem, Lindall, you just call us," Jaris assured her, turning and smiling at the girl.

Jaris pulled into the parking lot next to the apartment. He wasn't looking forward to another encounter with Denique, but he had to get Lindall safely inside the apartment. Jaris went into the building and up the steps with Lindall and hit the doorbell.

"I got a key," Lindall announced, unlocking the door. But he'd already rung the doorbell, and Denique appeared as Jaris and Lindall went in.

"Jaris brought me home, Denique," Lindall told her sister. "The party was awful. Kids were getting drunk, and I got scared."

Denique stood there, a towel wrapped around her head. She'd just washed her hair. She said flatly, "Thanks for bringing my sister home." She didn't even look at Jaris.

"Athena said Chelsea would be at the party, Denique, and all our friends," Lindall went on. "But they weren't, and the kids there were drinking and stuff. There were older guys, and I didn't know what to do. I tried to call Mom, but I couldn't get her. So I called the Spains, and Jaris came right away."

"What a bummer," Denique remarked, still not looking at Jaris. "But what can you expect around here? This is such a crummy place. People are all liars and stuff." Finally, she glanced at Jaris and asked, "Want a soda?"

"Sure," Jaris replied, not wanting to be impolite.

Denique pulled two root beers from the refrigerator and set them on the table. Jaris sat at one end of the table, and Denique sat at the other. They each took a sip and tried not to stare at each other.

"We've never lived in a neighborhood like this before," the girl stated. "I never knew that people like these ever existed. They're like some lower form of life. It's like we got on that TV show *Survivor* or something. I never met so many creeps in my life. Tubman High School—it's like my worst nightmare."

"Well," Jaris started slowly, "a lotta nice kids go there. You need to give it more time. It's hard being new at school. I know

146

it's bad having to leave your old neighborhood and your friends. But if you give it a chance, you might end up liking Tubman. My grandmother, she's got more money than my family does. She wanted to pay for me to go to a private school in Santa Barbara for my senior year. But I wouldn't even dream of leaving Tubman. I love the school."

"Boy, you made a bad choice," Denique sneered. "A private school in Santa Barbara! What an opportunity. That sounds like the school where I was going to go." Wistful sorrow came across her face.

"Denique, what I'm trying to say," Jaris insisted, "is that there are great kids at Tubman. I have some wonderful friends, and I hope that we stay friends all our lives. They got my back, and I got theirs. At lunch, we all go down to a special spot under the eucalyptus trees, and that's where we eat. If anybody's got a problem, we hash it out there. It's almost like a family."

"That guy Trevor Jenkins, he's one of your friends, isn't he?" Denique asked.

"Yeah, he's maybe the closest friend I got," Jaris replied, grinning. "We were little kids together in kindergarten. We got together after school, riding our big wheels, then our skateboards. I've known Trevor my whole life."

Jaris took a slug of root beer and then continued. "Nobody I trust more. He'd do anything for me, and I'd help him any way I could. He's like my brother. We couldn't be closer if we were blood relatives. I couldn't love the guy more."

Denique was now staring at Jaris as if she were seeing him for the first time. "I kinda like him too," she admitted.

Jaris was surprised at what Denique said. She seemed to have nothing good to say about anyone. He finished his drink, got up, and said, "Thanks for the root beer."

"Uh, thanks again for being there for Lindall," Denique responded. She didn't smile, but she didn't look mad either. That was an improvement.

Chelsea Spain went through four books on World War I poets. She had found out more about Wilfred Owen, as well as John McCrae, Rupert Brooke, and Alan Seeger. She was surprised at how much good stuff she dug up. It would improve her report, but she was still sad about missing the party. She was even sadder about maybe losing Athena as a friend. At school on Monday, all her friends would ask where she was and make fun of her for not coming.

Around five thirty, she put all her notes into her tote and got ready to ride her bike home. She should have been excited about all the fresh information she had gathered, but she felt forlorn. Athena's party should be breaking up about now. Everybody was probably hugging and saying it was the best party ever.

Chelsea loved her parents, but now she was mad at them. And Athena would probably be mad at Chelsea for a long time for missing her party. Heston Crawford might be mad at Chelsea too because he wanted to come to the party and be with her.

As Chelsea left the library, dark thoughts swirled in her mind, thoughts she didn't usually have. Pop—her beloved Pop—didn't really understand Athena, Chelsea thought. Just because she was kind of bold, he feared what she might do. That wasn't fair. Pop didn't understand about kids today. He was too old to understand. Adults who were around forty didn't understand people Chelsea's age, she thought. They were living in a different time. They were always afraid of stuff happening. But Chelsea and her friends were responsible. Even Athena wouldn't let anything bad happen at her big party. Chelsea was sure of that.

While she was inside the library, Chelsea had turned off her cell phone. The library rules called for that. But as soon as Chelsea stepped outside, she checked to see if she had any messages. There was one. It was from Keisha.

"Chelsea," Keisha said in the message, "call me the minute you can."

"Oh no," Chelsea thought. "She's gonna tell me all about the great party I missed."

Chelsea hit the speed dial for Keisha.

"Hi, Keisha," Chelsea said before Keisha had a chance to say anything. "Don't tell me! The party was awesome, and I missed everything!"

"Oh, Chel!" Keisha moaned. "I'm grounded for a month 'cause I lied to my parents about the party. They didn't want me to go. So I said the party was canceled and I was going to Athena's house to study!"

"How'd they find out?" Chelsea asked indignantly. "Did they spy on you, Keisha? I hope my parents never do anything so underhanded!"

"No, no!" Keisha answered brokenly. "It was the most horrible party I ever went to. Nobody I knew was there, except for Athena and Maurice and Lindall Giles. Inessa's parents wouldn't let her come.

And Falisha's mom wouldn't let her come. And there were these older guys—juniors—from Tubman. They brought beer and vodka and Margarita mix, and it was so gross, Chelsea. Athena got sick and was upchucking. Lindall got so scared she was crying and wailing like a baby. She ran outside and called *your* house for help!"

Chelsea turned numb. "My house?" she gasped.

"Yeah, and your brother and your father came to the house," Keisha told her. "Jaris, he took Lindall home. And your pop, he came roaring into the house like a madman, Chelsea. It was so terrible. Athena's mom wasn't there like she promised, and your pop went ballistic."

"Pop came in the house?" Chelsea gasped again.

"Oh, did he ever!" Keisha groaned. "He yelled at me and at everybody. He threatened to kick the sound equipment to pieces if we didn't shut it off. And he looked like he would've too. Everybody got real scared. Then he called Athena's mom, and he yelled at her too. He was like a wild man. He said if she didn't come home right away, he was calling the cops on her."

"Ohhh!" Chelsea sighed in horror. What would her father have done if he had found *her* at that party when she said she was going to the library? The thought gave Chelsea a nervous chill just to recall how close she came to doing just that. "Ohhh, Keisha!"

"And your pop," Keisha went on, "he made all the boys who were buzzed call their parents to come get them. And, Chelsea, that's not even the worst. I called Athena, and I couldn't get her. Her father said she was so sick from drinking the vodka that she had to go to the hospital."

"Oh my gosh!" Chelsea cried.

"You were so smart in not going, Chelsea," Keisha told her. "You said you'd go, and then you didn't. You were so smart. I wish I'd never gone."

Chelsea biked home after the call. When she got in the house, her parents were sitting at the kitchen table talking.

"Is Athena okay?" Chelsea asked. "Keisha just called me and said she had to go to the hospital."

"She needs to spend the night at the hospital," Mom answered sadly. "But she'll be okay."

"Ain't that nice?" Pop growled. "Ain't that beautiful? Your wonderful high school teacher, Trudy Edson, leadin' the younger generation on the road to perdition."

"What about Athena's father?" Mom asked. "He's got some responsibility too."

"Yeah," Pop agreed, "that's true. But the guy adores money. His thing is money. He's out there like a madman twenty-four-seven, makin' deals. He needs to sell that phony insurance to some more fools. Well, one o' these days he ain't gonna be closin' a deal. He's gonna be closin' the box on his little girl. Athena, she's in a bad place. Nobody lookin' out for her. Y'hear what I'm sayin'? She's a kid, and nobody's lookin' out for her."

Chelsea went into the living room and sank onto the sofa. She was facing Jaris, who was sitting in the easy chair. "I guess it was bad, huh, Jare?" she asked.

"Yeah," Jaris replied. "Poor little Lindall was scared silly."

"Is she okay?" Chelsea asked.

"Yeah," Jaris nodded. He was finishing up a text message. "She was crying and all that. I got her settled down. I warned her not to go to Athena's house. I told her Athena's a nice, goodhearted girl, but she's wild."

Jaris hit the send button and put the phone on the end table. He looked up at his sister.

"You know," he added, "I wasn't too happy about going in Lindall's house and facing Denique again. But she was okay this time. She even gave me a root beer. Denique even told me she liked Trevor. I was glad about that. Who knows what'll happen there."

Chelsea sank deeper in the sofa. "If I tell you something, Jare, will you promise to never, *ever* tell Mom and Pop?"

"Tell me what?" Jaris asked. "Okay, I promise."

"You know, when Mom and Pop wouldn't let me go to Athena's party," Chelsea began in a whisper, "I was so mad. I wanted to go so much. So I dreamed up this scheme. I thought I'd tell them I was going to the library to work on my project for history. But I was really planning to sneak over to Athena's party. Look, Jaris."

Chelsea pulled up her sweatshirt.

"I wore this cute top so I'd look nice at the party. I wanted to look good for Heston. I really was planning all day to sneak over to Athena's party. But then I got to the intersection on Iroquois Street, and I just couldn't do it. I was on the fence, Jaris, up until that last second. *I almost did it.* I almost fooled Mom and Pop and went to the party!"

"What made you decide to go to the library after all, chili pepper?" Jaris asked.

Chelsea leaned back on the sofa and sighed. When she spoke, she still spoke in a whisper. "It's weird, but it was something Athena once said. We were talking about our parents. Athena was going on and on about Pop being such a big wild guy who was always trying to protect me. Then she looked kinda sad. And she goes 'He loves you a lot.' Jare, I could tell she didn't think her father loves her all that much. You know what, Jaris? I was sitting on my bike on Iroquois Street, and I could see Pop's face. Not so much Mom's, but Pop's. I could see him all angry and stuff if he ever found out what I did."

Chelsea's eyes got big. Jaris knew what she was thinking and feeling about when Pop got mad.

"But something else too," she went on. "He'd be so *sad*. I mean, when you love somebody a whole lot and then they lie to you and stuff, I guess it must hurt a lot. I thought I couldn't hurt Pop like that."

Jaris nodded. "Well, good for you, chili pepper," he told her in a quiet voice.

"But I came that close," Chelsea squeaked, holding up two fingers with a small space between them. "I came *that* close."

"I've been there, Chelsea," Jaris assured her. "I've come that close to doing something very bad. *I mean, real bad.* What's important is that, at the last minute, you pulled back. It doesn't matter how close you got to the edge. What matters is that you didn't go over it."

Chelsea felt better that she confessed to Jaris. And Jaris made her feel even better still. But she was still worried about Athena.

"I hope Athena's okay," she said. "She's not bad or anything, Jaris. She's got one of the biggest hearts of anybody I know. She's my best friend. I don't know why she keeps doing dumb things. I really, really like her."

Jaris cocked his head a bit to think. Then he spoke, this time in a more conversational tone. "Maybe Athena does dumb things because deep in her heart she wants her mother or father to stop her. Maybe she figures if she pushes the envelope far enough, they'll get scared and have to stop her. Then that'll prove to her that they love her after all."

"I wish it'd work out for her, Jaris," Chelsea sighed.

"Yeah. Let's hope, chili pepper," Jaris told her. "Hey, did you score at the library, chili pepper?"

Chelsea smiled a little. "I got a bunch of good stuff. Some of it was sad 'cause these poets were so young when they died. But it was a beautiful kind of sad."

CHAPTER NINE

Trevor Jenkins sat in the back of the room in his first class. About two seats ahead was Denique Giles. He couldn't help noticing how those pretty, shiny curls caressed her long, lovely neck.

Hold on! He didn't want to go down this road again. He knew too well where it led—frustration, sadness, pain. He shouldn't be looking at pretty girls. There wasn't any one of them out there for him. It was like a penniless man looking in the window of a candy store. The candy might as well cost a million dollars because he didn't have a dime.

A couple of times when Trevor sat behind the gym to have lunch, Denique had joined him. But that didn't mean anything. She said something strange too. It was about calling her some weekend if he couldn't find anybody else to hang out with. Trevor thought about that several times, but he let it slip from his mind. He didn't need another kick in the teeth. Being lonely was a sad, dull pain. Having your hopes dashed was like a swift kick to the stomach.

Still … "If you ever want somebody to just hang with on the weekend," she had told him, "you could call me. I'd probably say yes." She had given him a little slip of paper. He almost threw it away several times, but he still had it. He transferred it from shirt pocket to shirt pocket, then to his wallet. He never got close to calling her. It had to be her little joke on him.

Tonight was Friday night. That day at school, Kevin Walker had invited Trevor to join him at a boxing match at the arena. Trevor knew Kevin would rather be doing something with his girlfriend, Carissa. But he asked Trevor because he felt sorry for him. Trevor didn't want to go to the fights, and he didn't want Kevin feeling sorry for him. Jaris had invited him to the Spain house for dinner. But he didn't feel like having dinner there, and he didn't want Jaris feeling sorry for him.

Trevor wanted to be out with a girl who really wanted to be with him. She didn't have to be crazy about him. She only had to want to have some fun with a guy who was okay.

At lunchtime, Trevor again went behind the gym to eat his lunch. His friends kept asking him why he stopped joining them under the eucalyptus trees. He gave them different lame excuses.

Maybe, Trevor thought, Denique would join him on the bench today. Maybe he'd have the nerve to ask her to go somewhere tonight. Tommy promised he could have the Cavalier.

Trevor waited for her, but she didn't come. He wasn't surprised. He was almost relieved. He'd worked himself up planning what to say to her if she came, and he knew he'd be hurt all over again when she said no. She might even laugh and say she didn't really mean what she said. Maybe she was only kidding when she gave him her phone number.

Trevor ate his ham and cheese sandwich, rolled up his lunch bag, and started getting up. There was no point to just sitting and staring into space. But as he was getting up, Denique appeared.

"You done with lunch?" she asked him.

"Yeah, but …" Trevor was about to say he'd gladly sit down again while she ate her lunch.

"I forgot my money for lunch," she explained.

"Hey, lemme buy you something," Trevor offered.

"Oh, please, no," Denique objected.

"Come on," Trevor urged, touching her elbow and gently guiding her toward the front of the building. They walked together, without talking, to the vending machines.

"Look at all the nice sandwiches," Trevor commented, trying to make conversation. "The ham and cheese is the best. Okay?"

He put the money into the slot, and the sandwich landed with a thud. Trevor smiled at her and put it in her hand. Then he bought two sodas, one for each of them. They walked back to the stone bench and sat down.

"I feel like one of those homeless people," Denique said. "Thanks for buying this. I really appreciate it, Trevor. I really am starved. I had some cereal this morning, but it's like eating air. There's nothing to those puffy things. Thanks for this."

She unwrapped the sandwich and took a big bite. "It *is* good," she remarked. "It tastes like real ham. Sometimes these sandwiches taste like cardboard."

"I hear ya," Trevor responded. "My mom used to pack tuna fish sandwiches for me every day. She insisted I eat them. My ma's a great lady, and I love her. But those sandwiches hadda be the worst on the planet. They were dry as dust, bitter as all get out, with just like a trace of mayo. I almost choked on the sandwich every day, but I ate it. I thought she'd find out if I didn't. Y'see, my ma's real tough. Then Ma got nicer. She said I could eat regular sandwiches if I wanted. That's loads better."

Denique laughed. Trevor had not seen her laugh much. She was a pretty girl, but when she laughed she was beautiful.

"By the way, that job application didn't go anywhere," Denique told Trevor, between sips of soda. "I called the Ice House about my application, and they said they didn't want me. I knew they wouldn't. Who wants a dummy with no experience?"

Trevor was about to tell her she was no dummy, but she spoke again.

"Wow, is this a good sandwich," Denique remarked. "I don't know how I forgot my lunch this morning. Mom always puts it on the counter for me and Lindall."

Trevor decided to keep quiet and let her do the talking. She seemed to have a lot to say.

"Trevor," she went on, "did you hear about the party Lindall got invited to on Saturday? She thought it'd be a nice girls' party, and it turned out some older boys brought booze. They were drinking and stuff. Lindall freaked. And you'd never guess what happened. Lindall called Chelsea Spain's house for help—Chelsea's her best friend. Anyway, you wouldn't believe who went and got Lindall from the party and brought her home. Jaris! That jerk, Jaris. He came in with Lindall, and *I had to thank him.*"

"Jaris is usually there when you need him," Trevor told her.

"He was pretty civilized actually," Denique commented. "We drank root beer, and he told me you guys were like brothers. Boy, is he sold on you, Trevor."

Trevor smiled. "Yeah, we're close," he agreed. "Always have been. I love the guy like a brother. Jaris is the kind of a guy who'd give you the shirt off his back if you needed it."

"Sort of like you, huh, Trevor?" Denique responded. "Buying a stupid girl a ham and cheese sandwich because she forgot her lunch money." She laughed. "But honestly, I couldn't believe the dude who brought Lindall home was the same jerk who laughed at me that day."

"Jaris is all right," Trevor said. "We all make mistakes."

Trevor's heart was racing. He wanted to ask Denique to go out with him tonight. He thought this was the right time. But then Denique looked very serious, and she started talking about something else.

"I want to tell you something, Trevor. I haven't told this to anybody, but I know you'll keep it between us. You know, my father ran out on us, and we lost our house and our car and everything. I hated him so much. He wouldn't pay child support or anything. He quit his engineer job—or so we thought. But, Trevor, we just found out something. It just about blew me away. We thought Dad quit his job so he could get out of paying us support. But he was laid off from his job months before we knew it. He was ashamed. He went off every day at the same time like he was going to work, but he was just sitting in the park."

"Poor guy," Trevor commented. "Sometimes when a man loses his job, it's like devastating, I guess. He feels awful in front of his family."

"Yeah," Denique responded, sipping her soda. "He had a nervous breakdown. He went to live with his parents, my grand-parents. Grandma, she's the one finally told us. He didn't want her to tell us. But it got so bad, he'd be sitting in his room all day and not even eating. It was like major de-pression, Trevor. I thought he was just a mean creep, but turns out he's sick."

"That'd explain what he did, Denique," Trevor told her.

"Yeah," Denique agreed. "I mean, I'm not glad to hear that my father is sick like that. But in a way, Trevor—do y'hear what I'm saying?—*I'm glad*. Because it means he didn't stop loving us. He stopped loving himself. He lost the will to live."

"I understand," Trevor said. "Maybe he'll get better, you know. They can help people like that now."

Denique didn't say anything, but his words seemed to be a comfort to her.

The afternoon classes were about to begin, and Trevor knew it was now or never. If he didn't ask Denique now, he might never do it. He was terrified that she might say no. And her rejection would plunge him once again into the pit of sorrow. Was he mistaking their casual friendship for something more? But he had to take the risk. One more time.

"Denique," he began, "would you like to maybe go someplace with me tonight? It's Friday and … "

His courage drained from him quickly. He was ready to turn away and run without even waiting for her reply. He had spoken the words so softly that maybe she didn't even hear them. That was all right.

He wanted to take the words back anyway. She was much too pretty to want to be with Trevor Jenkins.

"Why not?" Denique replied. "Like I need to spend another night looking at that hideous wallpaper in that apartment?"

"I'll ... I'll pick you up around seven, then," Trevor said. His heart was racing. He hoped he heard her right.

"Okay," Denique replied.

"Anyplace special you'd like to go?" Trevor asked her. He hadn't even thought things out this far. He hadn't expected her to say yes. His heart pounded so hard he thought he would have a heart attack. But at least he'd die happy because this chick had agreed to go out with him.

"Anywhere's good, Trevor," Denique answered casually. Then her face brightened. "Wow, you're really gonna take me out? I got something to look forward to. Is that cool or what? I like music, Trevor. Some little club or something. I like jazz and rock too. You pick the place." She was smiling now. "Thanks for asking me, Trevor."

Trevor couldn't believe what she'd just said.

"Thanks for asking me."

As they walked toward his afternoon classes, Trevor wondered whether it was all a dream. Maybe he had fallen asleep on the bench behind the gym. And he had this dream.

"Thanks for asking me."

That same day, right after school let out, Athena called Chelsea. She hadn't been in school all week. She was in the hospital for two days, and then she was home the whole week. Her mother had to take off time from classes to be with her.

"The doctor said I can come back to school on Monday," Athena said. "Chelsea, I'm going crazy here. Mom's so cranky. She says it's all my fault she had to skip all her important classes. I'm watching soaps all day, and it's awful."

"I'm sorry, Athena," Chelsea responded. "I'm sorry your party turned out bad."

"It was those two creeps, Vic and Nate," Athena told her. "They brought the booze. There wasn't supposed to be booze, Chel."

"Were your parents mad at you, Athena?" Chelsea asked. "You're not grounded or anything, are you?"

"No," Athena answered. "They don't do stuff like that, Chelsea. Mom said she's just sorry she has to stay home with me. But I'm feeling okay now. I'm ready to do something fun. You think Jaris would take us to the mall tomorrow? We could take the bus, but driving is funner."

"Hang on, Athena," Chelsea told her. She scooted to her brother's room.

"Jare, you doing anything special to-morrow?" she asked, her head poked in his bedroom doorway. "Like between maybe ten and noon?"

"Give me strength," Jaris groaned, rolling his eyes.

Chelsea went into Jaris's room and wrapped her arms around his neck. "Love you, Jare. I'll tell Athena it's on. Just a quick trip to the mall. Thanks loads."

"Okay, chili pepper," Jaris sighed.

"They're having this awesome sale on jeans, Jaris," Chelsea explained. She turned to go but wheeled back around to face him.

"Know what? Lindall has a crush on you," she told him. "You're her new hero. She told me that at school. She said you were the most handsome boy in the whole school. She's just so grateful how you helped her."

"Wonderful," Jaris responded.

"They got some Rocawear tees too, Jare, and they're soo cute."

She hurried back to Athena. "We're on, girl. Tomorrow between ten and noon."

Pop was coming down the hall. "Little girl, did I just hear you ravin' about you and the twit goin' somewhere?" he asked.

"Oh, Pop, Athena is feeling better, and Jaris offered to take us to the mall tomorrow morning," Chelsea answered.

"Listen, this is wonderful," Pop remarked. "This is the best news I've heard all day. Has she sworn off the vodka, or she gonna be carryin' a flask in her tote?"

Chelsea giggled. "Oh, Pop, she's so sorry about all that. She's never gonna let something like that happen again. Poor Athena, her party was ruined, and she got sick and everything."

"Lissen, little girl, my heart's bleedin' for her," Pop responded in mock sympathy. Chelsea ignored his comment.

"Jaris is gonna take us to the mall so we can get some skinny jeans," Chelsea told him.

"Not too skinny, little girl. Y'hear what I'm sayin'?" Pop commanded. He continued to the kitchen. Mom was making coffee.

"Want some coffee, babe?" Mom asked. "I need it bad. I'm beat. Greg has dumped more of his work on me. I don't know how much more of this I can take." Greg was Greg Maynard, her principal.

174

"Sure thing," Pop replied. "Always ready for joe." Pop sat down at the kitchen table. Sipping his coffee, he made a comment. "You know, Monie, I wish Chelsea didn't hang with that Athena all the time. She's a bad influence. I can't stand the kid."

"I know, Lorenzo," Mom agreed. "But I feel sorry for Athena. Chelsea is her only good friend, and, well, we can't break them up. Athena doesn't have a lot of good solid support at home, and Chelsea is especially important to her. It would hurt Chelsea to distance herself from Athena. And it would be a bad lesson for Chelsea—if somebody isn't perfect, dump them."

"Perfect I ain't askin' for," Pop complained. "But Athena, she's like a tickin' time bomb."

"I wouldn't let Chelsea go shopping with Athena alone anymore," Mom said. "But I don't worry when Jaris is with the girls, and he's agreed to take them, bless his heart. I know how he hates those shopping trips. Poor guy, he's bored out of his mind while those girls are running back and forth from the racks to the fitting rooms."

"Babe," Pop asked suddenly, "how'd we do it?" He had taken a swallow of coffee. Now he cradled the cup in his hand, a look of wonder on his face.

"Do what?" Mom asked. She poured another cup for herself and warmed up Pop's cup. She sat down at the table with her husband.

"Raise such good kids," Pop answered. "You're a smart lady, Monie, but you're one of those school teachers. Usually they don't know the first thing about raisin' good kids. They don't know from Adam how to take care of the kids under their own roof." Mom ignored the unintended insult. "And I'm a grease monkey. Whadda I know? My idea of discipline is yellin' my fool head off when somethin' goes wrong."

Pop took a gulp of coffee and went on. "I know I'm too strict sometimes, and I done plenty of dumb things. Like hangin' out at the bars after work in the old days.

But, Monie, Jaris is such a good guy. He's somebody I respect more than any guy I know, even if he wasn't my son. He's so good, so dependable. And little Chelsea. She's a firecracker, but look how she reached out to that little Lindall. That kid, Lindall, was a stranger without no friends. Chelsea takes her under her wing and brings her into the group of friends they got down there at Tubman. How'd we do it, girl?"

Mom smiled and kissed the top of Pop's head. "I guess we just loved them, babe. I guess we just loved them a lot, and they knew it," she answered.

At about the same time the same day, Trevor was jogging home from school. He sprinted over the fields and down the streets faster than usual. The days weren't so warm anymore. A nice cool breeze was blowing. Even though the blue would not fade from the sky for hours, you could see the outline of the moon. Trevor stopped for a minute and looked up at the moon. When night did come, it would turn golden like a disc of honey, spilling brightness across the sky.

Trevor continued his jog toward home. He didn't have a lot of good clothes, but he had a couple of nice things. He had a good blue shirt. Ma always said blue was his color. He'd wear the blue shirt tonight. He'd wear the good jeans, the ones that fit well.

Trevor had a lot of hope in his heart.

CHAPTER TEN

Trevor did not plan to tell his brother, Tommy, that tonight was a big deal for him. Trevor didn't want to have to explain if things didn't pan out. He was going to be cool and calm about tonight. He would act as though it was just a date with a friend— no more, no less. It was not some big romantic moment.

Still, after he got home and had his shower, Trevor asked his brother for a favor. "Tommy, you got any more of that aftershave lotion you give me before. I like the smell of that stuff."

"Sure, little bro," Tommy replied. "Use as much as you want." Tommy was grinning. "What's hap'nin', boy? You catch

yourself a hot one? You been keepin' se-
crets from your big brother?"

"Nothin' like that," Trevor objected.
"I'm going out with this chick. I got nothin'
better to do, and she's got nothin' better to
do. It's just killin' time, man."

Tommy continued to grin. "She hot,
man?"

Trevor smiled a little too. "She's hot all
right, but there's nothin' big goin' on."

"You need to wear a chick shirt, Trevor,"
Tommy advised. "I always liked that blue
shirt. You look good in blue. I hope it's not
in the wash."

"No, Ma washed it," Trevor replied.

"Hey, dude, I got a *new* blue shirt,
looks a lot better than yours," Tommy offered. "We're the same size. Why don't
you try it on?" Tommy seemed really
eager for this date to work out. He was
tired of seeing his little brother moping
around. He wanted to see him laughing
again. Tommy went to his closet and
brought out the shirt.

"Look, man, it's a knit tee. I wore it once, and the chick loved it. It's cool with these red pinstripes."

Trevor took the shirt. "Smells good," he remarked approvingly.

"You think I'd give you a dirty shirt, man," Tommy asked, laughing.

Trevor looked at himself in the mirror. "I don't even look like me. Feels good, Tommy. Thanks, man."

After Trevor slipped on his good jeans, Tommy tossed him the keys to the Cavalier. "Okay, dude, good luck," Tommy chuckled. "Remember, smile a lot, and listen to her. Chicks love to yak, and, when you listen, they like it. Whatever she's talkin' about, man, you act like that's the most interesting thing you ever heard. No matter what she's yakkin' about."

"Tommy, I appreciate how you're trying to help me out," Trevor told his brother. "But this is no big deal, dude. This is probably the only time we'll go out. She just wanted something to do tonight. She doesn't even like guys. But I ain't denying that it feels good to be going out, even though it won't lead nowhere."

Trevor walked out into the darkness toward the car. He knew he wasn't hot like Jaris or Kevin or Oliver. But he wore Tommy's cool blue shirt, he was wearing his good jeans, and he was driving a car rather than riding the bus. Maybe he had a chance for a second date. Maybe. Wearing Tommy's aftershave lotion, he didn't feel as dorky as he usually felt.

When Trevor got to Grant, he pulled up next to the apartment where Denique and her family lived. He saw the girl come out the door to the building. She'd been waiting in the lobby, behind the locked door. She looked hotter than she did at school, in a pretty skirt and a sparkling T-shirt. The clothes didn't look new, but they looked good on her. The minute she saw him, she started down the steps toward Trevor. But Trevor wanted to go inside and say hello to her mother. He thought that was the nice thing to do.

"Hey, Denique," Trevor greeted her. "You look nice."

"You don't look so bad yourself, Trevor," Denique responded. "I like your shirt."

"Thanks. Denique, is your mom home?" Trevor asked.

"Yeah," Denique replied with a surprised look on her face.

"I'd like to go upstairs and just say hi to her," Trevor said.

"Oh," Denique said, looking more surprised. "Okay."

Trevor followed Denique up the stairway and into the apartment. Mrs. Giles was sitting at the kitchen table on a worn chair, having a cup of coffee.

"Mrs. Giles, remember me?" Trevor asked. "We met the other night when I was worried about you walkin' home in the dark."

Mrs. Giles smiled. "Yes, I remember you, Trevor," she answered. "And I take that other bus you suggested. It's a much safer walk home when I'm working late."

"That's good. I just wanted to say me and your daughter are goin' out for a while," Trevor told the mom. "We'll be back maybe around eleven. She's a real nice girl, and I'm happy to be goin' out with her."

Mrs. Giles seemed astounded, but in a good way. "How sweet of you, Trevor," the woman remarked. "Denique, you said the boys at Tubman had no manners."

Denique giggled a little. "This one's different, Mom," she said.

Trevor and Denique then walked back down to the car.

"Trevor, do you *always* do that when you take a girl out?" Denique asked.

"Do what?" Trevor asked, holding the door for Denique.

"I mean, go and meet a girl's mom," Denique explained. "Most guys just pull up, hit the horn, and I go. Even where I used to live, where people had class, no boy ever went in to say hello to my mom."

"I hope it didn't bother you," Trevor replied. He started the car and pulled away from the curb. "My ma raised us that way. She's big on stuff like that. She said when a guy is takin' a girl out, he oughtta say something to her folks. Ma raised me with good manners. That's why my two oldest brothers make good soldiers. They were respectful even before they got to boot camp. They're used to being polite and doin' the right thing."

"What you did was nice, Trevor. Real nice," Denique commented.

They drove to a small club that catered to teenagers and twenty-somethings. The club didn't serve alcohol, but it served lattes, mochas, coffee, and carbonated drinks, along with fancy little desserts. It also had a lot of cutting-edge music. Alternative rock groups that hadn't established themselves yet played there. One group went on to snare a major contract, and they were now on the charts.

"Oh, I love the icy mocha," Denique remarked. "I love the whipped cream on the top. I don't care how many calories it's got.

It's heavenly. You don't think I'm fat, do you, Trevor?"

"No way," Trevor objected. "You're just right. You know, Denique, I never used to be able to afford comin' to a place like this and sorta splurgin'. Money was really tight around our house. Ma worked sometimes sixteen hours a day, but still the money didn't stretch. But now it's better. Ma doesn't have to work so hard. My brothers in the army are sending her money, and Tommy and me are helping out. I make pretty good money at the Chicken Shack. We got a tip jar there, and Neal, our boss, he's good about divvyin' the tips with us."

A girl and two guys began to perform.

"Ohhh, I like this!" Denique remarked. The guitar riff was smooth. "Most groups don't have a girl, but she's good."

Trevor looked at the two handsome dudes playing the guitar and drums. The girl was painfully skinny but pretty. Trevor noticed one of the guys in particular, the one on the guitar. He wore a tight T-shirt with a raunchy message on it. From the way Denique was looking at the dude, she noticed him too. When their set was over, Denique continued to sip her mocha.

"I wish I was as skinny as that chick, Trevor," Denique confessed. "She looked like she weighed maybe a hundred pounds. But the trouble is, I love to eat, especially mochas with whipped cream."

"I don't like it when a girl's too skinny, Denique," Trevor said. "I like a girl with curves—a healthy-lookin' chick, y'know?"

Denique smiled. "That one guy on the guitar, the one with the nasty T-shirt, he looks a bit like you, Trevor, but you're better looking."

"Me? Better lookin'?" Trevor asked in astonishment.

"You bet," Denique affirmed. "I couldn't believe a guy as cute as you could be so nice. Usually handsome dudes are smug jerks. There's this one guy at Tubman High, I don't know his last name, but his first name's Marko. He's very good-looking. But he's always got this smirk on his face, like he thinks the sun rises and falls on him. He came on to me like this was really my lucky day. What a fool!"

"Marko Lane," Trevor responded. Trevor dropped his head and shook it. He had a grin on his face. "He's got a big ego, yeah. He's really shocked when any chick turns him down."

The rock trio started another song. The girl wore a slinky, low-cut black dress. Some of the guys in the club yelled things at her. The drummer drummed louder to drown out the flirting.

The group played for about an hour. Trevor and Denique liked the group and listened as they played. Between numbers, they chatted about the kids at school and other everyday things. Trevor had no problem following his brother's advice: everything Denique said *was* the most important thing in the world to him.

When the set was over, Denique and Trevor walked out on the street. The night was beautiful and balmy. The summer warmth was having its last gasp before the fall chill set in. They decided to walk for a while.

The streets were full of people their age strolling. Most of the other young couples were either holding hands, or the guys had an arm around their girls' shoulders. Trevor walked beside Denique, but they weren't holding hands. After a few moments, Trevor felt something at his left hand. She had taken his hand. Trevor closed his fingers around her soft hand. It felt like velvet.

Chills ran up Trevor's spine. He couldn't believe she really liked him. He kept torturing himself with the fear that this was all some cruel illusion. What if Denique Giles was just in an unusual mood and she'd agreed to go out with him as a lark? What if it didn't mean anything to her? Tomorrow, things would be back to normal, and they'd just be acquaintances again. It would be like this night never happened.

"Trevor, do you know any married people, you know, who've been married a long time and they're really happy?" Denique asked him as they walked.

"Yeah. That guy Jaris's family for one," Trevor answered. "You should see his parents. They fight sometimes. But they're also like teenagers sometimes, just dancin' with each other, huggin' each other up. They kiss real hot, Denique, like kids. I saw 'em once when I was at the house. Mrs. Spain's a school teacher, real smart and professional, and he's a rough talkin' auto mechanic. But they got some chemistry goin' there, I'll tell you. Alonee's parents are happy too. But lotta kids at Tubman come from busted families."

"My parents were okay, I guess," Denique responded. "They weren't like real happy or anything, but it was okay. Then my father lost his job. I guess he couldn't face telling Mom and stuff, and he just went to pieces."

They sauntered for a few moments without talking.

"When I get married," Denique announced, "I want it to be like that guy Jaris's parents. I want to be in love forever and ever. I wanna be able to tell him anything. I want him to be able to tell me what's in his heart too."

Trevor laughed at her little-girl excitement. "I think maybe a big secret is to never grow up all the way," Trevor suggested. "Jaris's pop, especially, he's like a wild little boy. I read in a book once that when you grow up, your heart dies."

They'd been strolling a while, and the street had become all but empty.

"I don't want my heart to die, not ever," Denique declared. Then she glanced up at the sky. "Oh, Trevor, look at the moon, how big and yellow it is! There's a yellowish glow around it."

"Yeah," Trevor said.

Denique turned to Trevor. "Are you a good kisser?" she asked him.

Trevor felt his face turn warm. "I … I don't know. I haven't kissed that many girls," he stammered. He grew very nervous.

Denique planted her hands on Trevor's shoulders, stood on tiptoe, and brought his face closer to hers. She kissed Trevor on the lips, and he kissed her back, but it wasn't a quick kiss. They held it for a long time.

"Wow!" Denique gasped.

Trevor didn't know what to say. He felt as if he had been transported to another world, one with no troubles or cares. When they walked on, Trevor's arm was snugly around the girl's shoulders, and her arm was around his waist.

Anyone seeing them would say they were lovers.

Back home that night, Trevor tried hard not to awaken his brother. Tommy slept in the same room on the other side of a make-shift plywood wall. But Tommy whispered, "How'd it go, man?"

"I ... uh ... put your shirt in the hamper, Tommy," Trevor replied. "Thanks for loanin' it to me."

Tommy poked his head around the divider. "How'd it go, dude?" he demanded. Then a big smile broke out on his face. He hadn't seen Trevor grinning like that in ages. "*That good*, huh?" Tommy laughed.

"Tommy," Trevor said softly, almost in awe, "she was so wonderful. I think Denique really likes me, and I like her so much. Oh man, this is the best night of my whole life." But dark clouds formed almost immediately. "I hope she wasn't just pretendin'."

"Dude, you want me to come over there and smack your head upside down?" Tommy threatened.

Trevor fell back on his pillow. Even when he closed his eyes, he saw her. He saw the dark curls around her oval face. He saw her lovely figure. Maybe she had a few more pounds than she wanted, but she was all the more lovely and beautiful to him. She was perfect.

In the dark silence, Trevor kept thinking, "Make it be real. Make it be real this time. …"

Right before lunch, Jaris Spain and Sereeta Prince had a meeting with their AP American History class teacher. They were both relieved that Ms. McDowell had approved their recent updates. Jaris had worried himself sick that he wasn't up to par in the AP class, but he was getting stronger with each stage. It looked now as though he would get college credit for the course. Jaris wasn't a great student. He had to work like a dog to earn the grades that came easily to kids like Oliver Randall and even to Sereeta. But if Jaris got college credit for this class, his goal of doing well in college and becoming a teacher became more realistic.

Outside the classroom, Jaris and Sereeta hugged and congratulated each other.

"We did it, babe!" Jaris exclaimed. "Course, I knew you would, but me …"

"There you go," Sereeta laughed, "selling yourself short again. I think Ms. McDowell wrote more good things on your paper than she did on mine."

They walked off, hands joined. Jaris couldn't wait to go down the little trail toward the eucalyptus trees. He was bursting to share the good news with his friends.

The gang called "Alonee's posse" was already assembled when Jaris and Sereeta appeared.

"We both scored!" Jaris announced.

"Way to go!" Alonee responded. Oliver Randall was with her.

He smiled and added, "Didn't I tell you that you could handle it, Jaris?"

Derrick Shaw and his girlfriend, Destini, were eating their sandwiches, and they high-fived Jaris and Sereeta.

Kevin Walker and Carissa Polson were just arriving. Carissa tripped coming down the trail, and Kevin had to catch her. He made the most of it, holding her in a tight embrace and kissing her. Kevin grinned shyly and told her, "That's my reward for catching you, baby."

Sami Archer was there with Matson Malloy, and they laughed.

Then Trevor Jenkins appeared, with a girl beside him. Trevor knew the trail leading down to the eucalyptus trees could be slippery. So he held on tightly to Denique's hand. Everyone's head was turned toward the couple. Everyone was silent.

"This is Denique Giles," Trevor announced, "my girlfriend." The others introduced themselves. When Kevin introduced himself, Denique looked at Kevin with a mock grimace, and he grinned at her.

"Hey," Sami declared, "welcome to the club, girl. Trevor ain't been around in a while, and we were missin' him. Now here he's back in the fold, and he's bringing a hot little chick along with him. Way to go, Trev."

Denique giggled. She sat down on the grass next to Trevor. She glanced over at Jaris and Kevin and admitted, "I guess it *was* kind of funny, you guys. And it was a lucky split for me. If it hadn't of happened, I'd probably never have met this wonderful guy." Denique looked over at Trevor and smiled.

Everybody lifted whatever they were drinking—orange juice cartons, soda pop cans, and thermos jugs—in a toast. "Here's to Denique's cheap pair of shorts and to our buddies Trevor and Denique."

The group resumed their lunch and conversation. But Trevor fell silent. He was hoping Tommy was right; that there's a girl for every guy. Denique was his girl now, and he hoped she'd be his girl forever. But who knew?

"For now, at least," Trevor thought, "she's the one for me."